A BEARER

of

DIVINE REVELATION

A Bearer of Divine Revelation

NEW AND SELECTED STORIES

Lawrence Dorr

William B. Eerdmans Publishing Company

Grand Rapids, Michigan / Cambridge, U.K.

Wm. B. Eerdmans Publishing Co.
255 Jefferson Ave. S.E., Grand Rapids, Michigan 49503 /
P.O. Box 163, Cambridge CB3 9PU U.K.

Printed in the United States of America

08 07 06 05 04 03   7 6 5 4 3 2 1

Library of Congress Cataloging-in-Publication Data

Dorr, Lawrence.
A bearer of divine revelation / Lawrence Dorr.
p.   cm.
ISBN 0-8028-2123-5 (pbk.)
1. Title.
PS3554.069B43   2003
813'.54 — dc21

2003054325

www.eerdmans.com

For Margaret Clare,

the constant angel of His presence

Contents

Introduction

Lawrence Dorr has been writing fiction in English for more than forty years; this most recent gathering of his short stories follows three earlier collections: *A Slow, Soft River* (1974), *The Immigrant* (1976), and *A Slight Momentary Affliction* (1987). More than half of the fifteen stories that make up *A Bearer of Divine Revelation* come from the earlier collections, but their appearance here gives them new focus and new life. Taken together, these fifteen stories allow the reader to discover not only Dorr's mastery of his chosen genre but also the larger pattern in which he wants these stories to be understood.

Readers who already know Lawrence Dorr know that Lawrence Dorr is the pen name adopted by a Hungarian survivor of the disasters that visited Hungary before, during, and after World War II. Born in Hungary in 1925, Dorr has lived in the United States since the 1950s, but before that he had experienced the life of an exile or an alien in Hungary, Russia, Austria, and England. (Corbin Scott Carnell's introduction to *A Slow, Soft River* provides the basic biographical information about these years, and about his transition to American life and culture.) And even his fifty years in the United States have not diminished Dorr's awareness of being a foreigner, an outsider, someone from Eastern Europe.

Eastern Europe has, for more than a century, been an alternative

source of knowledge about Europe, the West, and the human soul —
knowledge about the impact of world wars, about totalitarianisms,
about the Holocaust, about the powerful attractions of irrational
forces, about life after the dissolution of the Soviet empire, about despair and hope. For many of us, our sense of the current historical and
cultural situation has been shaped at least in part by the contributions
of Eastern European writers — from Poland (Jerzy Kosinski and
Czeslaw Milosz), the Czech Republic (Franz Kafka, Václav Havel, and
Milan Kundera), Hungary (Arthur Koestler), Romania (Elie Wiesel),
and Croatia (Slavenka Drakulic). They have taught us much of what we
know about our personal and political selves and about our situation,
about the murderous twentieth century and its aftermath, knowledge
of our dreams and our nightmares we should find it hard to do without, although usually we manage to keep this knowledge at a comfort-
able distance.

But Lawrence Dorr, having lived through much of the same Eastern European history as the writers I've just mentioned, tells us what
he knows in ways that set him apart from the others; what he has
learned also sets him apart. The stories collected in *A Bearer of Divine
Revelation* bear testimony to what can be and has been lost. But they
bear testimony to what can be recovered as well.

It's deceptively easy to describe the larger narrative structure of
these stories. If we focus on Dorr's various narrators, for instance, we
find that they are recognizable versions of one basic narrator, a young
man born in Hungary, raised as a Calvinist in a largely Catholic culture,
who walked more or less innocently into the destructive energies of
Eastern Europe in the 1930s. Some critics have described this compos-
ite narrator as an exile; others see a Job or a survivor, come to bear witness to what he has suffered. As this young man grows into his adult
years, he experiences the dissolution of family, national sovereignty,
religious certainty, the verities of his boyhood education, and the alle-
giances of personal and social relationships of all sorts. The early stories of this collection systematically strip away the cultural infrastruc-

ture as well as the personal pieties. Like Job, like Everyman, like Ivan Ilyich, the character is left to discover what remains when almost everything has been lost. Whether it is the example of a strong and heroic father, the *noblesse oblige* of a wealthy and cultured aristocracy, the teachings of the church and of the academy, the love of friends and of comrades-at-arms, the virtue of a just cause — nothing is exempt from the terrible corrosions of pre-war Hungary, World War II itself, and the Soviet aftermath.

But these stories do not move on next to consider what can be made of a diminished thing. Instead, much of what the early stories take away is restored, at least in part, in the stories that follow. Health, work, dignity, love, family, faith, peace, and happiness re-enter the world of the narrator, albeit gradually. Nothing suggests that Dorr thinks that these gains make up for or cancel out the earlier losses, but all is not loss, and Dorr seems to insist that the gains are gains, not illusions.

What is notable and striking about Dorr for many readers is his bold practice of describing these losses and reappearances not only in the drama of persons, ideologies, and causes, but also in explicit references to the outward features or manifestations of spiritual and religious life — a shaft of light, the shape of a cross, bits of Scripture, fragments of the Latin mass, references to works of art, icons, crucifixes, liturgy, hymns, and sacraments. Dorr unapologetically brings these features into his stories, boldly assuming that such things exist in the world and therefore exert small and large influences on people, at expected and unexpected moments. Moreover, the confident but naïve young Hungarian at the beginning of these stories becomes very attentive to other traditions as the stories proceed. It is remarkable what this young Calvinist can learn from Russian Orthodoxy, Greek Orthodoxy, and Anglo-Catholicism. It is remarkable what role a phrase from the Latin mass, or light filtered through stained glass, or the shadow of a crucifix can have in these stories, or how much life is revealed in a woodland scene, a fish in the bottom of a boat, a rabbit running for its life.

Dorr holds to at least one more bold set of assumptions: made in God's image, we humans are built for beauty, for delight, for pleasure. Made in God's image, we are meant for community, for communion, for love. Made in God's image, we make and keep promises; we are meant for obedience and service, and for the prospering and thriving that accompany such faithfulness. We are meant for joy. As these fifteen stories move from youth to old age, from exile to homecoming, this set of assumptions moves from memory to hope, from hope to belief, and finally from belief to fact. With this view of human time and divine intention, Lawrence Dorr has earned our attention. And these stories should earn him the broader readership that he so richly deserves.

JAMES VANDEN BOSCH

A BEARER

of

DIVINE REVELATION

An Act of Admiration

I was fifteen the summer of '36. To me Hitler was no more than the stub of a pencil held to my upper lip to make my sister laugh. This was the summer of the Berlin Olympic Games, of Jesse Owens.

As usual in the summer, we were at our villa, fifty kilometers from Budapest. Standing on our front terrace, we could see the Danube, wide and olive green. Four kilometers upriver, the far side belonged to the Czechs. I could not see them, but I knew that they were there. I was never allowed to forget, at home or at school, that in 1920 at Trianon a slice of Hungary had been given to the Czechs. That summer the Czechs themselves would not let me forget it. A Czech station was beaming a Hungarian language broadcast telling me that I'd better stop dreaming and wake up to the fact that not one grain of Czech soil would ever be handed back to Hungary. No one else in the house listened to it. I sat alone in the room with its cheerful blue peasant furniture and hand-painted plates and jugs, hating the traitor's sneering voice. On the terrace I could see Mother with a Tyrolean straw hat on her head, cutting flowers, and I could hear the guests shouting back and forth to each other as they lay in deck chairs under large striped umbrellas, playing a memory game. They talked endlessly about music and art. They were not interested in Justice and Honor.

Near the staircase leading to the upper rooms, the guns, rifles and carbines, hung against green felt. Solomon, Father's retriever, slept under this staircase. In his sleep he looked as wise as the plaster casts of philosophers at school. We were both waiting for the guests to leave, to have Father back with us: his real self in boots and cord breeches and khaki shirt, following Solomon in the woods, teaching me to walk quietly, to observe and even to smell things. After we had shot and skinned the meat, we would sit awhile, he smoking a cigarette and I scratching Solomon's head, and he would tell me about the War.

The sneering voice stopped, and there began a babble in Czech. I turned off the radio and went upstairs and out through the back door across the bridge that led to the back terraces. There was nobody to share my hate. I walked up to the red water tank and climbed on top. I used to play Tarzan here, jumping off the tank to catch the nearest branch of the walnut, but with the sneering voice in my ears I didn't feel like Tarzan. I wondered if I were brave enough to offer my life for my country like Father did, but I wasn't sure. Then I heard Peter whistle our signal, and I jumped off the water tank. Peter was my best friend in the summer. He had accepted me even though I was three years younger and I didn't smoke or earn money. He was the only boy in the village who called me by my Christian name. The others always shut up when I came along.

"I thought you'd gone deaf," he said, standing at the other side of the fence.

"Come over."

He climbed the fence. He was a head shorter than I, and blond, with almost white patches where the sun had bleached his hair.

"I saw you standing on top of the water tank," he said, sitting down on a stump. "Were you playing Tarzan?"

"No. I don't play anymore."

"That's good. Only little boys play. You are as big as a horse." He watched me from the corner of his eyes. I couldn't hit him because be would go off and leave me. Besides, Father told me one didn't hit anyone weaker than one's self. I didn't say anything.

"I've been away." He plucked out a blade of grass and looked at it.

"Where?"

"I don't know if I should tell you."

"You don't have to." I sat down to make myself smaller.

"I will if you promise not to tell anybody."

"On my honor." We shook hands.

"I've been away in training with Captain Feher," he said. I burst out laughing.

"Don't laugh. He is a very good captain."

"How can Mr. Feher be a real captain like Father?"

"Not a captain like him," Peter agreed. "Captain Feher is only a Free Corps captain, but he knows how to fight. We are going over tonight."

I stood up. "Across the river?"

"Yes."

"Have you got a uniform and all?"

"Yes. And we are paid much more than the regular soldiers."

"Tonight?"

"Tonight," he said.

"I am going with you. You know I can hit anything with a .22."

"You are too young, Laszlo. We won't be shooting at rabbits; we'll be shooting at Czech soldiers."

"They are much bigger."

"You can't come. You haven't been trained. There isn't any uniform for you." With his arms out he looked like Cicero in our history book.

"Peter, you go and tell Mr. Feher that I am going with him because — "

"You can't just send messages to Captain Feher."

" — because he'll need me. I've been over twice. I wanted to see how they look."

"Did you see them?"

"No, but I saw their pillboxes from a distance. You can't see them from our side. I know where they are. Tell Mr. Feher that I don't want any pay, but I'll need a rifle."

"Can't you bring one with you?"

"No. I'd have to ask Father."

"Why can't you just take a rifle? He wouldn't miss it at night."

"That would be like stealing."

"All right, I'll tell Captain Feher," Peter said. "We meet at ten sharp, beyond the village, by the stone cross. Get yourself some dark clothes." He climbed the fence and began to run. I went back down to the house, to my room to ransack my wardrobe. In the end I decided the dark brown Red Indian suit and moccasins Mother brought me from Paris would do. I spent the afternoon cutting off the red felt fringes.

*   *   *

I got out of bed, already dressed, at a quarter to ten, pulled on my moccasins, and left the house over the bridge. I didn't need to be especially quiet, for the grownups were singing. I recognized Mother and her friend Anna, the opera singer, yoo-hooing at each other in a duet. I climbed the fence by the second terrace. From somewhere Solomon came to see me off.

In ten minutes I had reached the main street of the village. It rose slightly here as the road curved over a stream. I crossed the bridge. Below me tiny silver crosses vibrated on a motionless black ribbon. Most of the houses were dark. Somewhere a drunk began to sing. As he passed the houses, the village dogs, one by one, started to bark, until a woman's shrill voice cut the singing short. The invisible drunk cursed; then a door banged shut. The frogs took over again.

Even before I could see the stone cross I knew that they were already there. I felt it somehow, and I could smell them. The very poor, who lived in caves at the far end of the village, always smelled sour. I took two more steps and stopped. A torch thrust a white beam into my face; then I heard Mr. Feher.

"Boys, our gentleman guide has arrived." There were sniggers. The white beam dropped away from my face to the ground, making a narrow line leading to the cross.

"Come here!"

I went, wishing that Father was here with me. Nobody ever sniggered around Father.

"Good evening," I said. Again, sniggers were coming from the dark.

"I don't expect you to salute me properly like a soldier," Mr. Feher said, "but I warn you, we are not playing games. Now, tell me; is it true that you have been over?"

"Yes, it is true."

"Don't lie to me." He put the light on my face.

"I give you my word of honor." As I said this, somebody laughed aloud. Mr. Feher turned.

"Shut up," he said. "Do you want to come with me, Laszlo?"

"Yes, sir."

"Good." He put his torch down on the base of the cross beside some flowers. They were soft and bent, dying. "I want you to write on this paper, Laszlo, that you come of your own free will. . . . Good. Another question. Have you anything in your pockets that would identify you?"

"No, sir."

"Good. From now on you'll be called Number Twenty-five. And you call me Captain Feher."

"Yes, sir."

"All right. Give him a rifle. The rifles are not loaded. I'll give the order to load."

It was Peter who handed me the rifle, an ammunition belt, and a bayonet. The rifle was an old .256 Mannlicher. We had two of them at home. I pulled the bolt back.

"What are you doing, Twenty-five?"

"I am checking my rifle."

"I told you it wasn't loaded."

"Yes, Captain Feher. My father told me I should trust only my own eyes and fingers with any weapon in my hands."

"Fall in!" he barked. "Extinguish your cigarettes. If I catch any of you smoking, I'll smash his toes with his own rifle."

We started on the four-kilometer hike in single file.

*   *   *

We rested awhile on the shore behind a large weeping willow. Two boats were hidden under the tree. Peter lay on his back beside me, pretending that I wasn't there. I had fixed my sights with a white thread and reached for his rifle to fix his sights too, when Mr. Feher asked me what I was doing. I told him that Father had taught me this and that we always did it when shooting in the dark. Mr. Feher took my spool of white thread and threw it away, calling me a seamstress. I wondered if the others would talk to me now that I was called Twenty-five. They whispered among themselves.

A black cloud covered the stars.

"All right," Mr. Feher said.

We loaded our rifles, and the boats were pushed out onto the river. Two men rowed in each boat. The oars dipped silently, and we seemed to be floating above the water. In the dark I could smell everything separately: the trees on the shore behind us, the river, the men in the boat, our rifles, and the boudoir smell from the collar of my Indian blouse where my sister had once poured some of Mother's perfume.

"Are you scared?" Peter whispered into my ear. I shook my head. I was afraid of many things: our Latin teacher at school, the mad woman of the village with her large goiter and strange running walk, the whirlpool close to the dock where the head gardener's son had died; but there was nothing frightening in tonight. I was happy. Darkness was safe, Father had told me. One just had to lie down and keep still. I was

8

safe here. And if I got shot, that would just make me more like Father. He had two wounds from the War.

"Watch your oars," Mr. Feher whispered in the other boat. The denser blackness of the shoreline rushed out at us; then the first boat crunched on it. We came in much more quietly.

"Twenty-five," Mr. Feher whispered.

"Sir?"

"Who do you want to go with you?"

"I ask for a volunteer," I said. Father had silenced the Russian observation post with volunteers.

"Keep your voice down. Who wants to go with Twenty-five?"

Peter volunteered. I knew he would.

"All right. You go to the pillboxes, close enough to find out how they are manned, then come back and report to me. Understand?"

"Yes, sir."

"Leave your rifles here."

We moved slowly in the dark, like a war party of Indians. I could just feel the branches touching my face. Indians always knew where they were going, and they were patient. I knew where the pillboxes were, and I was patient. I halted for a moment to listen. Peter bumped into me.

"What is it?" he whispered.

"Nothing. I was just listening."

"Go on, Twenty-five," he said. We went on. Soon I found a path. It was a shy, unobtrusive path, winding between trees and bushes. It felt safe walking on it. I began to jog, holding down the bayonet with my hand.

The trees suddenly fell away. The stars were out again and the pillboxes were there, just across the field. I was looking at them, feeling exactly as Father must have felt when he crawled out from the trench knowing that the whole regiment watched him. The pillboxes were real, and I was real.

"You've seen them, Laszlo," Peter whispered. "Let's go back."

"What would Captain Feher do to you if we don't find out how they are manned?" I crawled out onto the field. I was completely soaked by the heavy dew. Peter followed me.

It was a long crawl. The muscles in my neck began to ache. I told myself I shouldn't mind because this was a part of soldiering. Then we reached the first pillbox and it was all right again. In the silence I heard the river. They were close to the shore, camouflaged by green grass to hide them from us on the other side.

The first pillbox was empty. Even the squat steel door stood open. There was no machine gun inside. We checked them all. They were all empty. I felt like a little boy playing at soldiering. I turned angrily and started back across the field. Peter pulled me down. Then I saw it, too: a white house, further back inland on a mound partly hidden by trees. We took cover and waited.

"I hope they have no dog," Peter whispered.

"We can find out. You bark, Peter. You bark better than anyone I know."

"I can't. Not now."

We fell silent. A soldier appeared. I could see him against the house. Then another. The smaller one lit a cigarette. They were talking.

"It's real. After all, it's real."

"Shut up," Peter whispered. "Shut up!"

The guards went on talking. I knew what to do. When Father saw the Russian observation post, he took one of his men with him and silenced the guards; then they surrounded it. The Russians came out with their hands held high, and the Russian officer handed Father his revolver. Father offered him a cigarette. They shook hands.

The smaller guard pitched his cigarette away and disappeared behind the house. The big one lit up now and, shielding the cigarette in his hand, turned to go to the other side.

"We're going up there."

"What for?"

"To silence the guards."

"No," Peter said.

"We can't go back otherwise." The night had faded. The exposed side of the house had lost its clean contour and washed into the background.

"What'll we do?" Peter asked, eyes on the house.

"We'll go up there and silence the guards. I told you."

"Kill them?"

"We don't kill. I'll bang them over the head with the bayonet. Then you go back and get Captain Feher to surround the house and we take the Czechs prisoners." I started off walking, bent over. I was in a hurry, afraid that Mr. Feher might move up and spoil everything. He wouldn't know what to do in a situation like this. He hadn't been in the Great War. Peter followed me. At the foot of the mound we got down on our stomachs and crawled up to a position behind a tree. We waited.

The big guard walked by. He smelled of tobacco and soldier smell, but he didn't move smartly like a soldier. He went up to the front of the house and called out to the other guard in a loud whisper. An answer came back but not the little guard. He must have sat down behind the house. I was thrilled to hear them speak in a language I couldn't understand. This was real. Father had taught me to say "hands up" in Russian, but I wasn't sure if the Czechs would understand Russian, and besides, I couldn't frighten them without a rifle.

The big guard turned and walked back. He came close by the tree, stopped and yawned, then went on. I stood up. Now he wasn't so much bigger than I. His back was very wide. I lifted the sheathed bayonet. He stopped again and leaned forward a little. It felt like bringing down an ax the wrong way. It jarred my arm. His cloth army cap fell backward; then he pitched on his head with a thud. His falling rifle made another noise. Peter came and dragged him down behind our tree.

"What'll we do now?" Peter sounded strange.

"Unsheathe your bayonet. Put its point against his heart. If he wakes up, he'll feel it and won't dare move. Do you know where his heart is?"

"Yes." He had the bayonet in his hand.

I crept around the house. The smaller guard was sitting on the ground, propped against a tree trunk. He looked little and tired, but he was armed with a rifle. I banged him over the head. He moaned. I lifted him under his armpits and dragged him around the house to our tree.

"Peter!"

He didn't answer.

"Peter!"

I let the little guard down. Peter was sitting beside the big guard with his head bowed, rubbing his hands on the grass. He was crying.

"Peter!"

"I didn't mean to do it. He moved."

"Peter, there are more of them in the house — "

"I didn't mean to do it."

"You must go back to Captain Feher and bring him here. Tell them to come quietly. There are more in the house."

"I can't go without my bayonet."

I pulled it out and gave it to him. He got up and left. I moved the little guard behind another tree and sat down beside him. I looked at his alien uniform. He was a Czech soldier. And so was the other. Enemies. Both of them. Czechs with sneering voices. It began to go round and round. I couldn't get off. I felt sick.

The little guard was sitting up, looking at the naked bayonet in my hand. I didn't remember unsheathing it.

"Lie down," I said in Hungarian.

He lay down.

"You speak Hungarian!"

"My people were Hungarian," the man said, "but when I grew up this was already Czechoslovakia. . . . What happened to Ladislau?"

"He is dead."

The little man covered his face with his hands.

"He didn't mean to kill him. You must understand."

"We're not at war."

"He didn't mean to kill him."

The little guard didn't say anything.

"How many are there in the house?"

"Fourteen. What'll happen to them?"

"We'll keep them prisoner till we go home. I am sorry that I can't offer you a cigarette."

"Aren't you too young to smoke?"

"Get up. I'll walk you past the house."

"I'd rather you kill me while I'm lying down," he said. "It would be worse walking away, waiting for it."

"I'll turn you loose, but you must go away from here and not talk to anyone. There are more of us coming up soon, and they might want to lock you in, too. You must go far from here."

"I will."

"Give me your word of honor."

"All right."

He gave me his hand. It was calloused and limp, and he was sweating. I don't know why but it made me remember the flowers on the base of the stone cross.

*   *   *

By the time I got back, Mr. Feher was coming up the mound with his men. One of them gave me my rifle. The white thread was ripped away from the sights. They surrounded the house. Mr. Feher beckoned to me.

"You did a good job, Laszlo. Did your father teach you how to do it?"

"Yes, sir."

"You and I go in now." He took the gun from its holster. "You can learn a few things from me yet."

I clicked off the safety and followed him. He opened the door and stepped back. Nothing happened. We went in. Mr. Feher turned on his torch. There were men sleeping on cots ranged along one side of the room. On the opposite wall hung rifles. Mr. Feher grabbed the nearest sleeper and shook him. The man sat up and said something in Czech.

"Speak Hungarian," Mr. Feher shouted. The man just shook his head.

"Anybody speak Hungarian?"

I was covering them with my rifle. They didn't seem to want to get out of their cots.

"I speak Hungarian," a blond fellow said.

"Tell them that the house is surrounded. They are to get up and line up by their beds." The man translated. "Tell them to keep their mouths shut. . . . Why is there nobody at the pillboxes?"

"We are not at war with anybody yet," the interpreter answered. "We have no machine guns for them."

The fourteen men lined up by their cots. In their underclothes they did not look like Czech soldiers. They looked like people.

"I want more light," Mr. Feher said. The interpreter lit a gasoline lamp and pumped it up. They were looking at us. Nobody said a word. The lamp hissed like an angry gander.

Mr. Feher called in six of his men.

"Two of you take the rifles and ammunition outside. The rest watch the prisoners. You come with me, Laszlo."

I followed him outside. He had not offered any cigarettes and he had not shaken hands. It was no honor serving under him. I wanted to go home.

"Laszlo, we have to plan the next step together. You'll understand what I am getting at. You are not a stinking peasant like my men." He laughed. I didn't say anything. Father would never call a peasant stinking.

"Are you listening to me?" Mr. Feher growled.

"Yes, sir."

"You knew how to silence the guards. You understand the necessity — "

"We didn't mean to hurt him."

"I expected a different answer from you. Do you understand that we can't take prisoners?"

"No, sir."

"What would you do with them?"

"I would keep them in the house with two guards. We can lock them in when we leave. . . . And I would free the man who speaks Hungarian."

"Why?"

"Because he is our brother. We don't want him to hate us."

Mr. Feher leaned against a tree and laughed. "D'you think it matters how he feels about us? The only thing that matters is who is stronger. That man is in Czech uniform. This isn't your father's kind of war. The Gentlemen's War lost us a big part of our country. Think about it."

He walked past me and called the men outside to gather around him. Morning breeze came from the woods. The trees sighed. I was sure he wouldn't do it in daylight.

"As I told you," Mr. Feher said, standing in the center of the half circle, "the Free Corps doesn't take prisoners. Our safety demands this. We don't ask for mercy and we don't give mercy. If one of these bastards escapes from the house, we can expect the whole Czech Army at our back. We'd be lined up and shot." Mr. Feher waited. Peter glanced behind him. All the others looked behind them. It was morning now.

Mr. Feher went on. "I don't want to attract the enemy with rifle shots. It has to be a quiet job with the bayonet. One by one, like pig killing. Any volunteers?"

Nobody moved.

"I offer five pengoes, extra, from my own pocket."

"Number Nine humbly reports."

"All right," Mr. Feher said. "Number Nine, take up position by the door. The rest, line up facing the door. I'll make men out of you yet."

Mr. Feher went inside the house. We lined up in double order and waited. When he came out he stood in front of us, a bit to the side, and called us to attention.

"Let's begin," he commanded.

The interpreter came outside, and the door shut behind him. His uniform was unbuttoned, his hair uncombed. He had forgotten to put on his cap. Seeing us, he stiffened.

"Did you tell them to come out one by one to be searched?" Mr. Feher asked.

"Yes, sir," the interpreter said.

"All right. Go ahead and search him."

The man lifted his hands high and waited. Number Nine stepped behind him. The bayonet sliding in between his ribs went so fast that be died before registering pain. Number Nine dragged the dead man's body to the side of the house. He cleaned off his bayonet on the dead man's jacket and went back to stand by the closed door.

"Next one," Mr. Feher called.

The door opened and a man stepped out. He lifted his arms high and waited. A question appeared on his face as if he were listening to a faraway sound. Then his knees buckled. Number Nine pulled him over beside the first one and cleaned off his bayonet.

"Next one," Mr. Feher called.

The door opened. A man stepped out and lifted his arms high. The door closed. He stood still; then his knees buckled. Number Nine worked with the not-too-slow, not-too-fast rhythm of a woodcutter.

First there had been a man's face and his disheveled hair. Then came the man whose face asked a question. The next one was not a man; he was an automaton, an automaton whose hair color and whose face I could not remember. Was he tall or short? The door opened and shut. It was a soft sound, and the automatons kept coming, looking alike. There must be more to it because this couldn't be all; but they kept coming out looking alike. They all held up their hands before their knees buckled. I looked at the others. They stood at attention in their green Free Corps coveralls, chest out, hands flat at their sides, like soldiers. I too stood at attention, thinking of Father, the way he stood when the band played the national anthem, but I couldn't do it right. The Indian suit was brown but it wasn't real because real Indians dressed in leather.

The sound was not angry, not like the time I slammed the door on my sister. My legs felt boneless, and I looked down and noticed that I had left on two red-felt fringes. I ripped them off. Nobody noticed, and it made my knees feel better and it stopped me from hearing the soft sound. I counted up to twenty before it came again. The next time I counted very slowly up to thirty. It wasn't fair to count too fast. I looked at one of them because there must be more to it than this. I wanted to remember a face, but all I could see was fear. I closed my eyes. I counted to sixty, then stopped because I had to take a breath.

"Next one."

The door did not open.

"Next one," Mr. Feher shouted hoarsely. "Next one."

The door opened and one of the guards came out. "There are no more in here, Captain Feher," he said.

"At ease!" Mr. Feher commanded.

*   *   *

We hid the boats under the weeping willow. All the time, rowing back, we had tried not to look at each other. Mr. Feher said that we were dismissed. He told us to disperse at ten-minute intervals. I pulled back the bolt on the rifle and took out the clip, then took off the belt with the bayonet and handed them back to Mr. Feher. He wouldn't take them. I laid them at his feet. He didn't say anything, just looked at me. I turned around and walked away.

On the highway there were always people coming and going and saying, "God give you a good day," so I kept to the shore. Soon I was out of sight of Mr. Feher and began to run. The grass felt good to my feet, and the sandy patches, and even the willows whipping my face now and then felt good. When I was a little boy my Indian name had been Swift Feet. Sometimes, to myself, I was still Swift Feet. I had been here only last week, jogging along at the wolf trot, feeling the same grass under my feet. I stopped running. I looked for signs as I walked by the Big Chief trees I knew, but they were the same as usual, tall and stately, the greatest among their people.

The side-wheeler *Tahi* was coming upriver. She always came between ten-fifteen and ten-thirty. I couldn't tell time by the sun like Peter. He had learned it when he was young and took care of goats.

I passed the abandoned brick kiln and reached the backs of the village houses. I tried to think of breakfast; I tried to think of Trianon, of Injustice, of Our Brothers in Subjugation, of Honor. I tried to think of what Father had said about his return from the War, but I remembered only the tall chimney of the kiln, as it had come down two summers ago. One minute it stood above almost everything; then the supporting trestles at one side of the undermined base burned through, and the chimney fell. First slowly, unbelieving that its time had come, still higher than the church steeple, then faster and faster, rushing down. When the dust settled, there were only broken pieces of brick scattered on the ground. I wanted to think like a soldier, but kept on thinking like me.

I took the shortcut through the woods, running all the way to our high stone wall with its wrought-iron gate. I was breathing so hard that it sounded as if I were crying. For the first time in my life I didn't know what I wanted to be. I could always pretend to be anybody I liked, but now I couldn't even pretend to be my yesterday me.

Solomon scented me and started a racket behind the gate. I went inside. He jumped on me and licked my neck, then went down to sniff around my moccasins. He was finding out where I had been. I took the left-hand stairs and walked along the first terrace. Everything was quiet. Mother must have taken the guests for a walk. I came level with the terrace and saw Father sitting alone in a deck chair under an umbrella, reading.

"Good morning, Father," I said, and walked past him.

"You must have been up early, Laszlo . . . Laszlo!"

"Yes, Father?"

He looked at me, then swung a leg over the deck chair and stood up.

"Anything the matter?"

"No."

"Let's go up to your room," Father said, leading the way into the house and up the stairs. He stopped in front of my door. I opened it.

"Come in, Father."

He came in. "You haven't slept in your bed," he said.

"No, I haven't."

"You can always tell me if you want to go out at night. We always trusted each other."

"Yes."

"When did you go out?"

"Last night."

We stood in the middle of my room. The polka-dot curtains on the window were fluttering like ducks just out of a pond.

"Where did you go?"

"I'd rather not tell you."

"I am asking you."

"I went over the river with Mr. Feher and his Free Corps."

He took a step toward me. "Is that man mad? Once a thing like that starts, God only knows where it will end. And you, going with them!" His eyes were hard, but he kept his voice down. "What is the purpose of a Free Corps? To kill unsuspecting people, then run back home feeling like heroes? Tell me."

"To kill Czechs." When I said this, Father pressed his hand to his head as if he were slicking down his hair.

"Because Czechs are not people with four limbs as we are? Because they have no mothers and fathers and children as we have?"

I couldn't answer. I saw them again, standing in their underclothes beside their cots, looking like people.

"Have you . . . have any of the Czechs been killed?"

The plum tree outside the window was humming with bees. Cook was singing in the kitchen.

"Yes."

"What made you go with them?" His question was a great shout that filled the room, hardly leaving me any space to breathe.

"I wanted to be like you, Father."

He knocked me down. I waited on the floor, hoping that he'd bring his riding crop and beat me so hard that I could be forgiven tomorrow. But he didn't beat me. He picked me up from the floor and held me against his chest. I heard him murmur, "Lord, what have I done?"

"You didn't hit me hard, Father. I don't feel it at all."

He didn't listen to me. He said it again, out loud now, and I felt his chest vibrate with each word.

The Binge

He watched his sister's tight grip on the receiver. It gave her hand the color of the winter apples they bombarded each other with as children. The sun coming through the curtains made her hair light up. The windowpanes were taped with large Xs. She put the receiver down.

"Bad?"

"He is dying," she said.

"I have to see him."

"You can't. The railway lines are bombed, and it would take days to get there." She was her practical big-sister self. "You can't leave now. You have your orders."

"What can I do?"

"She asks you to pray for Father."

"Me?"

"She knows how I — "

"Yes," he interrupted, not wanting to hear his sister say it out loud, defining her disbelief, and so build a huge, empty edifice of hopelessness. They were both saved from saying anything more. Planes were coming toward Budapest, and the air-raid sirens began to moan.

When it was over, he went out to the street directly from the shelter. Halted yellow streetcars were dotting the main artery like prehistoric creatures mired in quicksand, already dead. He walked fast, conscious of his black riding boots, one of his father's special presents. Everything he had ever given him was special: the cigar-box truck his father made for him on his sister's birthday when he had felt left out; that "If God is for us, who is against us?"; that Hungary was the most beautiful country in the world, yet it was conceivable that a French woman like their mother would think otherwise; the first rifle. They were all special presents because they came from him.

Somewhere, across the Danube on the Pest side, fire trucks and ambulances were screaming. With an almost automatic stocktaking, he once more compiled the list of friends living over there.

*   *   *

The church, antithesis of anything that might suggest Rome, stood close to a park of well-trimmed grass and tamed, captive chestnut trees in solitary confinement. Each had an iron fence around its base that reached up a few feet, making the trees look like giraffes in a zoo. Walking up the church steps, it occurred to him that he had never really prayed for his father before. He was always included, but more out of politeness than a feeling that he needed to be prayed for. He simply and always WAS.

The church door was made of varnished oak. He put his hand on the wrought-iron doorknob and turned it. The door was locked. He shivered with fright, his body seeming already to know what his mind would not accept, not yet anyway, casting about desperately like a starving fisherman, only to come up with a wriggling poison-fish. He turned and ran down the stairs, his boots noisily clomping, then dampened by the thick, orderly, Calvinist grass. He passed the imprisoned trees, grinding now the gravel on the walk where trusting little boys, coming up out of their air-raid shelters, played ball, not knowing anything about the black cloud of predestination that had already marked them. He crossed the street, slowing down to a walk because people were looking at him, a lieutenant in the tank corps. He was twenty-one. He went on searching for an open door. A place for a rehearing, anywhere now.

A huge cross faced him, almost as if to bar his way. With abhorrence he saw the bleeding, twisted body of Jesus hanging from it, looking like the dead who were dug up after the raids. The dead Kristus, as if resurrection had never been. Kneeling down — he who had never knelt in his life and who looked down on the papist, idol-worshipping, incense-burning majority of his countrymen and his own French mother with the amused tolerance of a Westerner meeting a prayer-wheel-spinning lama — he was not certain if he had not by this one act compounded all his sins into a super wrong.

"Our Father," he said; then he stopped. He wanted his own father. There was nobody who could take his place. "Don't take away our father, Oh Lord God," he prayed.

Somebody came into the church. He got up and went outside, halted by the strong sunshine. He noticed the women in their summer dresses floating by him, their buttocks and breasts moving with tiny motions that took his breath away and caused his chest to ache with longing for all of them. Four more days, he thought, and I'll be sent to the Front. The perfect thing to say to a woman to be loved quickly. And it was the truth.

Away from the church a question mark grew into a snake that curled around his father's chest to strangle the beating heart. There was no more sun in the sky, no streets, houses, roofless walls with staring, empty eyes, no women, no desire, merely the endless gray ribbon of the sidewalk cut by chasms into which he stepped, deaf to the blaring of cars and the clanking of streetcar bells. *When people died under them, they were covered with sheets of brown paper.* But he came up again and again onto the gray ribbon.

The incense smell didn't bother him anymore. It was cool inside and, as soon as he knelt down, peaceful. Too cool and too peaceful for the question-mark snake to enter. He knelt silently. There was no need to say out loud, "Don't take away our father, Oh Lord God." He was resting safely on his knees. When he got up, he was a happy man just recovered from a grave illness.

It did not last long. Like a drunk in search of the next bar, he stumbled from church to church, till, remembering the morning's raid, he crossed over the Danube to Pest. The morning's raid made the black smoke rise up straight, then rejected, bent under the clouds, gray now, then nothing. Air. Golden-blue summer air that had been a house with people in it.

They used to row a long way up the Danube. The green river was hemmed in on both sides by wheat fields. Golden-yellow. When a breeze was blowing, they could smell the ripeness of the kernels, and there was always a sound like a contented sigh.

The air-raid sirens began to howl. The shelter he took was in an ornate nineteenth-century apartment house. The helmeted air-raid warden standing outside saluted him.

"This is a lucky shelter, Lieutenant. Glad to have you, sir."

"Thank you." Lazily he touched his cap, playing his role of a "line officer home for a brief spell" for the warden. To keep it up, he one-two-three-foured the length of the stone floor, then down the grimy stairs to a narrow corridor formed by the dividing iron fence. The door hung open, waiting for him. He stepped inside and stopped, forgetting his self-appointed role. There was an electric bulb hanging from the vaulted ceiling like a single fruit of a dried out, dead vine. It gave out shadows that turned people's faces into a set of bones. They sat on backless benches, each with a suitcase or a box, as if waiting for a train.

"Sit down, Lieutenant," somebody said. He sat down among them and touched his face, feeling the bones. I must be like them, he thought. He watched an old woman lying on a cot with her arms folded over her chest. She looked at him and shivered. Without a bag, a box, or a suitcase, he alone was naked. Nobody spoke.

Then the sound came. First like the susurration of tiny, feathered wings, then whistling with increasing frenzy till the bang of explosion shook the building. The light swung side to side like a railwayman's lamp. Another one. It walked on iron-shod feet, shaking the earth, coming closer. In the dark a child whimpered.

Not much longer now, he thought, wondering how that other pain would feel.

The light came back on. A woman with her head on the bench was kneeling as if at a confessional, her bent back asking for mercy. The earth stopped shaking.

The All-Clear sounded. He rushed up the stairs, across the hall, past the warden standing at the door with his steel helmet hanging from his arm like a shopping basket, down the street, running by a caved-in house where people were digging with ineffectual frenzy. He stepped over a body that the explosion had smashed against a wall, the brain, flesh, blood, and bones mixed in a pulp with bits of clothing. He went around a mountain of brick where a leg stuck out, bent at the shin. There was no street to go on. Turning back he walked slowly, for the first time noticing the thick white dust on his black boots. Uncle Joseph was bigger than his father, but he fitted into an urn the size of a pound tobacco can. Ashes to ashes. There was nothing now. He walked on. As in a delirious dream he stepped on a street sign, halted, bent down, read it twice, went on, came back to read it again. It was the street where the woman in the wine-colored dressing gown lived, had lived two weeks ago, the two of them together. An urgent, hungry cannibalism on his part and a betrayal on hers that chance had arranged and that allowed him to shake himself dry like a dog coming in out of the rain, but now it was the only thought that did not hurt. He was running again, running toward an untouched house, through the hall, surrounded by echoes of his own footsteps. He stopped to push the dead bell, never for a moment doubting that she was there behind the door. He banged on it till the door opened and he rushed in, not hearing her say, "What is it? What is it?" to hold her close, to feel her body against his.

"Let me close the door," she said, leaving him. "I thought I'd never see you again." She watched his face, his eyes, then she asked it again: "What is it?"

In four more days, he wanted to say, I'll be at the Front, but instead heard himself blurt out, "My father is dying."

"And you came here?"

"I saw the smoke in the morning." They were still standing in the narrow entrance like polite strangers, apart but attentive.

"You want me?"

He didn't answer. Just looked at her.

"You need me." It was a statement.

This time he saw her with eyes that wanted to memorize, photograph her ivory skin, her long limbs, her heavy breasts pulling away from each other, her face, one cheek buried in the pillow, showing her profile cameolike. Gently he turned her head, looking down at her closed eyes, her trembling mouth.

"I would like to stay with you always," he said. He noticed then that she was crying.

*   *   *

After he left her house, he stopped to phone home. His sister answered. Hearing her voice, he knew. He stepped out of the phone booth to look up at the sky and shout *Take me, take me,* but his open mouth was mute, as if his vocal cords had been ripped out. He knew that "If God is for us, who is against us?" But if God was against you.... The soundless words asked for American planes and bombs and death. Nothing came. The sky was overcast that night.

The Noise Was Heard Afar Off

The narrow windows on the sides of the van were covered. The only light, anemic, almost stillborn, came from the air vent on the roof. The ventilator was the type that turned with the wind pressure. There were cracks in the floorboards. He could smell the exhaust fumes. Sitting on the wooden bench, he pretended he was in a movie house where the operator had run out of films and was turning an empty projector. The screen was filled with light, then dark, light, dark, light. The empty projector was quite logical, considering that Budapest had been under siege for five months. It was very important to him to know that he was still thinking logically.

From across the river artillery fired. He could hear the shells going overhead and then exploding. The Russians were shelling the old Maria Theresa Palace. The Germans had turned it into a stronghold.

The van bounced on the cobblestones; then the driver downshifted. The engine began to whine on the steep climb. He didn't know where they were going. They were all fastened to a long, shiny chain either by the right or the left wrist. Nobody spoke or looked at each other, not even in the dimness of the van. He remembered Uncle Emil and how hard it had been to talk to him or even to look at him toward the end. Uncle Emil had had a terminal illness. All of them in the van were to be executed.

The van stopped with a jerk, the worn-out brake shoes scraping on the drums. The Russian artillery fired again, the shells whistling overhead, giving a strangely reassuring sound. Then the van's door was wrenched open, and the light was pouring in, hard and blunt, pushing against his eyes, reflecting the cold snow that made their chain glitter like a silver fruit bowl; then the first man was stepping through the door, pulling the chain and all the rest of them behind him, and he heard the shouting outside, "'raus, 'raus," and the chain was uncoiling, pulling his left wrist. Stepping down from the van, he saw the SS, dirty, unshaven, their guns pointing at him.

"Dear God," he said. He was looking up at the building, at the inscription he had seen every school day of his life: MONUMENTUM AERE PERENNIUS. He was eleven when he first saw it and read his first Latin sentence: *Italia a peninsula est.*

The soldiers close to the van were still shouting "'raus, 'raus." The men on the chain entered the building. He was the sixth, shuffling up the wide, shallow, worn-down steps, warm after the bitter cold outside, climbing to the first floor and the second, thinking that not so long ago, at the age of eighteen, he had graduated from here and was part of the "walk" that had taken them in single file, singing "Gaudeamus igitur," all over the school.

The third floor was damaged. The plaster was knocked off, revealing the old bricks and confuting the proud inscription outside: this monument was *not* more lasting than bronze. As a school, it had lasted just over a hundred years. He wondered how many of the old boys were here again. They always met somewhere. Two of them had been at the Military Academy with him. They graduated as lieutenants and were sent to the Eastern Front. Both of them died in the Ukraine during the retreat. There was nothing extraordinary in that; people died in wars. The extraordinary, the unexpected, had happened when he went home at the end of August. He told nobody about the leave, not even his family, fearing a jinx, yet the day after he arrived home he received a phone call from his friend Tibor, who was supposed to be in the western part of Hungary with an anti-aircraft unit. Tibor had wanted them to meet that same afternoon in a café on the Buda side of Chain Bridge close to the tunnel that led up to Maria Theresa Palace, which the Budapest natives called the Fort. The Chain Bridge was the oldest of the bridges connecting Buda and Pest.

He had arrived at the café first and, enjoying the sun, decided to stay outside. Tibor had been his best friend since school days, when they were the only Calvinists in a class of forty-two divided between Jews and Roman Catholics. When all the others had religious instruction, the two of them built paper airplanes in the school yard. In the spring they always tried to fly their planes through the open classroom windows.

Sitting down at one of the small marble-topped tables, he faced two of Chain Bridge's four stone lions. From where he was sitting he could look into one lion's open, empty mouth. Their creator had forgotten to carve tongues in their mouths and had committed suicide when the omission was noticed by a passing bootmaker's apprentice. He doubted that anybody would commit suicide now because of an artistic failure. The people sitting all around him drinking beer or coffee or vermouth were pretending that the war was far away, though everybody knew that the Red Army was closing in, that the Arrow Cross had added revenge killings to its ideological murderings of Jews in anticipation of their defeat, that there were more Allied bombings, and that the German army had taken over the palace after arresting the Regent of Hungary.

He felt strange sitting here in peace, when four days ago, gasping with exhaustion and fear, he had been fighting through rings of Russians and Germans, fighting not for any cause or ideal but because he wanted to come home, he wanted to live if for nothing else than to watch women walk by, women who were not refugees yet, women who did not walk with bent, defeated shoulders and who did not look at the world with the desperate eyes of stray dogs.

His friend Tibor came into view. He passed the right-hand-side lion and stopped suddenly. Three Arrow Cross members with drawn guns were pressing a Hungarian soldier against the stone pedestal of the left-hand-side lion. The shots were not loud.

Tibor crossed the road and sat down opposite him. The Arrow Cross men were looking at the people sitting on the café's terrace. Nobody moved or looked back at them. They turned and left.

"What's going on?" He was not looking at Tibor; he was looking at the soldier lying in a motionless heap against the base of the stone pedestal. This was Budapest. He was on two weeks' leave.

"The Arrow Cross has decided you are AWOL after twenty-four hours," Tibor said, "and will shoot you on the spot."

The older of the two waiters went inside. The telephone was just inside the open doorway.

"I have two weeks' leave. I am safe."

"Yes," Tibor said. "We know that."

Tibor never explained who the "we" were or how they knew about his leave. Instead they talked about school days, Professor Beresztoczy, the teacher in charge of their class, girls, sports; then, without a pause, Tibor asked him to deliver a sealed envelope. The contents would enable a man to disappear into safety. The man was important to the non-Communist underground.

The older waiter cleared the table next to them, then went inside again.

"I think you ought to know that the man you'll be saving is one of our pastors," Tibor said.

A slate-gray truck stopped by the left-hand-side lion. Two men got out of the cab, lifted the corpse onto the truckbed, then drove off.

An hour later he had gone to the address and handed over the envelope. There were two things he remembered about the apartment: the silver fruit bowl on a cedar chest in the hallway and a cracked mirror on the wall. When he handed over the envelope, the man lifted his hand in a gesture that was half blessing, half good-bye. Neither of them had said a word.

There were still five days left of his leave when he was arrested.

*   *   *

The urinal had the same overpowering smell of creosote he remembered from school days. What was new was the cigarette butts all over the floor; smoking in the lavatory could have meant dismissal from school.

German cigarette butts looked different from the Hungarian ones. The tobacco was a lighter color. He hadn't smoked since September, when the first interrogator had offered him a friendly cigarette.

The old man standing next to him had trouble undoing his fly. He was attached to the chain by his right hand. The guard kicked him. The old man fell against the creosoted wall; then the chain tightened again and they were out in the corridor. The lower part of the wall was still painted green and still smelled of school. He remembered Professor Beresztoczy telling him here in this same corridor that without logic one can't orient oneself in the world but there was no logic left anywhere and it was no use to pretend anymore.

He wondered if they would be fed before the hanging.

*   *   *

He was off the chain, lying on the floor, alone. The classroom — he recognized it as his sixth-form room, where they had started reading Cicero — had been partitioned into small cells. He waited for them to come and take him to the interrogators, but when the guard came, he brought a bowl of potato soup, a chunk of black bread, and two blankets.

They were condemned already, the guard said. There was no need for interrogation. The Germans were no sadists.

The soup was warm and it filled him with the same thankfulness he always felt at Communion, when he was certain of the Presence all

31

around him and he knew a completeness that he could not explain. He wasn't really cold now or hungry, and because there would be no more interrogations he wouldn't have to hear his own shrieking that had turned all existence into pain that he would do anything to stop.

Toward morning he was awakened and moved to the next cell. The occupant, along with two others, had been taken downstairs. One of them was the old man. He could smell the creosote.

*   *   *

Artillery fire was spaced like a watchdog's bark in the morning, but the sounds of Russian small arms increased with the light. This cell was on the window side of the classroom where little Acel, the mathematical genius, had sat in the first row.

He wanted to sleep but was hungry again and the lice had started to bite him between the shoulder blades. He got up to rub his back against the jutting corner of the windowsill. Through the mesh-covered window he could see the playing fields; the goalposts had been moved and were lined up beside each other, forming a long, continuous gibbet. The three were there, hanging grotesquely, their heads lolling to one side, reminding him of the plucked chickens in the window of a kosher butcher shop he used to pass on his way to violin lessons. A shop that had frightened him with its strange, hard, alien writing. The old man had the largest sign pinned on his chest telling about his crime. He couldn't read it. Usually it said TREASON.

The light was gray, suffused with the cold, hungry misery of the world, enshrouding the three hanging there, swinging with a barely perceptible, leisurely movement. He remembered the trees at the side of the playing fields, the sound they had made in the slightest breeze. There were only stumps now, mute and accusing, pointing at the sky.

He wasn't afraid of death. He was afraid of suffocation, the slow choking, the kicking legs that would turn him into a toad.

There was more small-arms fire close by. A German machine gun opened up with hysterical chatter; then there was an explosion and silence.

His head felt as if it would burst. He felt his lungs heave and saw black dots before his eyes. Desperately, he clenched his bowels, trying not to give in to this final humiliation when he already had an image of himself with which he could barely cope: an image of a coward lying motionless in the corner of a cell in the Margit Street Military Detention Center, watching the Arrow Cross armbands with their sharpened, degraded crosses, fantasizing about Roentgen eyes that could penetrate envelopes so that he could tell them his pastor's *nom de guerre*, his food-coupon number, and his "vital" occupation, and so stop pain. He hated his best friend, Tibor, his brother who didn't trust him enough and sealed the documents in an envelope. And he hated his own parents, who had taught him the sanctity of a sealed envelope, and he hated the man he had set out to save, whose savior he had become because he was not able to betray him. The Arrow Cross had put themselves beyond the circle of God, where mercy did not exist; he had been taken to the wharf, to the frozen Danube, to watch some of his old classmates, Jews, stripped naked and shot — to refresh his memory, they had said, but it didn't. It couldn't.

He went to the corner of his cell and defecated. It didn't matter anymore. He would be taken down today. Beyond the choking was God and mercy and peace.

A Russian T-34 was clattering down the street. There was tommy-gun fire in short bursts on the first floor and the second; then it all stopped. Somebody was running down his own corridor in hobnailed boots, stopping long enough to fling open his cell door. It was the SS guard who had brought him the potato soup and the black bread, racing toward the back staircase.

He left his cell and locked the door behind him, then opened the other third-floor cell doors. Most of the men looked like discarded rags flung against the wall. Their eyes were gleaming. They didn't speak to him.

On the second and first floors everybody was dead. There was no food in any of the cells. None of the dead had saved any bread in their pockets.

On the street the dead horses had already been picked clean. The Russians were going on toward the palace. The civilians who had emerged from the ruins were suspiciously watching each other. They were all watching him, looking at his filthy uniform.

Three gaunt women emerged from one of the ruins. They still had the yellow stars on their breasts. Their faces were the waxy white of the dead. They stared at the people collecting on the street, some pushing baby carriages loaded with furniture, some dragging suit-cases. More Russians passed in horse-drawn wagons. The three women with their yellow stars began to smile and wave and call out to them. The other civilians were sullen, afraid of the Russians, two of whom got off one of the wagons and walked toward the three gaunt women, grinning with stainless-steel teeth. More Russians joined them. In a moment the women were surrounded. He couldn't see them anymore but he could hear their screams above the shouting of the Russians and he began to run among the ruins, not knowing where he was going or even why he was running, knowing only that the burden he carried was unbearable. He wanted God and mercy and peace. He ran on, stumbling on broken bricks and masonry, but he could still hear the sound of their screaming.

Brandenburg Concerto

He sat on a boxcar's floor with his legs outstretched, leaning against the wall wrapped in one of the Brandenburg concertos, feeling content. The music was alive and intimate and nothing else existed beyond it. It had been very difficult for him to start it playing in his head, but once he could remember the sound of the Ruggieri violin, piccolo tuned, the rest came easily. By the time the concerto reached the first Menuett, he swayed with the music, the back of his head rolling from left to right, right to left on the side of the boxcar. Even the crack around the sliding door turned white as if the music had become visible, bringing in light.

"Lieutenant," the girl, an ancient twenty-three-year-old bone collection with short, comical, dead hair, called to him, "how far are we from Budapest?"

"I don't know," he said, angry at her for shutting off the music. Now he had to limp with the rhythm of the boxcar and remember that just an hour ago, when the train had stopped, this same skin-and-bone creature had been raped by three Russian soldiers. They had pushed the sliding door back and climbed in, flashing around with a battery light. One of them kicked him aside and then raped the girl. It would have been very simple had they not kept the light on the girl's face. Her eyes had been like glass eyes. Not frightened or accusing or anything.

Just dead. "I don't know," he said again, feeling guilty for his anger. "I really don't know."

"I believe you, lieutenant," she said.

"Call me Peter."

"Thank you."

"What is your name?"

"Sarah. I am back from Auschwitz."

Auschwitz didn't mean anything to him. A town in Germany or Austria.

"Do you like Bach?" There was no answer, so he repeated the question. "Do you like Bach?"

"Yes," she said in a small voice.

"Are you crying?"

"No," she said. He reached out for her hand. A little, rough, narrow hand.

"You are crying now," he said, moving closer to her.

"I am lousy."

"Who isn't?" He put his arm around her bony shoulders and eased her head onto his chest. She didn't weigh more than a rabbit. "My mother used to enjoy just reading the score."

"I like Bach," she said, wonder in her voice. The snoring of the sergeant at the other end of the boxcar stopped with a moan. Peter could hear the music again. The limping rhythm changed to a pleasant swaying.

"Can you hear it too?" he asked. Then his heart jumped, but it was all right. She wasn't dead. She was just sleeping. Peter kept on swaying; then he too dropped off.

The noise of the sliding door being pushed back woke him. The sergeant was looking at him apologetically.

"I'm thinking of getting off, sir. It's not healthy for us around stations."

"I am in no shape to do any jumping, sergeant, but you go ahead."

"Sir!"

"Yes?"

"Just wanted to say, sir, that I am pleased to have served under you." He delivered his speech standing at attention. Peter squirmed a little. The girl was pressing on his leg.

"You were like an uncle to me, sergeant," he said, hoping he gave something too.

"Do you have your crutch handy, sir?"

"Yes. Don't worry about me, sergeant. They won't take a man who can't even walk properly."

"You'll be all right, sir, after a while, but I don't like to leave you."

"All right, sergeant, jump."

"God be with you, sir."

"God be with you."

He saw him drop from the open door. The limping rhythm was the same again, then changed to the minute thunder of a bowling alley as the train crossed another track, then again the limping. The variety of sounds made the train seem to go faster.

The girl woke up.

"We are almost at home," Peter said. "I recognized the rubbish dumps. They are still here . . . ."

"What will happen to you when we arrive?" the girl asked, her eyes on Peter's right leg.

"I don't know."

"What's the matter with your leg?"

"It's my thigh. The fragment, or whatever it is, is pressing on the bone. It doesn't hurt if I don't step on it."

"You'll have to go to a hospital. . . . I was a medical student before They took us away."

"Then you must be older than I am."

The girl ignored this. "Didn't you have doctors in the Army?"

"The doctors had no time to really fix it. We were pressed very hard. I was left behind to take care of myself." He looked toward the open door and added, "The sergeant decided to stay with me."

"He must have loved you."

"Who?"

"Your sergeant."

"He had enough of war."

"Maybe if you stay with me," the girl said. "I am Jewish, and the Russians fought the Nazis."

"Stay with you?"

"You'll be safe."

"Safe?"

"Yes." But she began to cry. "I am a little bit crazy."

"Everything will be all right when the war ends. Where are your mother and father?"

"They are dead. Have you got anybody?"

"My mother and my sister, I think. We live on the Buda side. You can stay with us."

"Me?"

"Yes. You like Bach." They both laughed.

"You are good," the girl said. "I never thought. . . ."

"Thought what?"

"I never thought that I'd ever want to speak to you."

"Speak to me?"

"If you had been herded like . . . like. . . ."

"I was at the Front. I wasn't doing it. My family didn't approve. . . ."

"But you knew at least some of it. And you were not one of us when. . . ."

"That's true."

"I like you, anyway."

"You are a good Christian."

"I am not even a good Jew," the girl said. "I don't believe in a God who can let things like this happen. Can you?"

With loud clanking the cars bounced against each other like billiard balls; then, after a final convulsion, the train stopped. The girl was at the door looking out; then the next minute the air was rent by the firing of automatic weapons. Peter, lying on his side, heard the girl shout "What is it?" then voices answering back. Now there was firing all around them. The girl was kneeling beside him, trying to get him up, but he wouldn't move, not as long as he heard the tommy guns' rattling.

"The end of the war," the girl shouted. He stood up, leaning on his crutch, the sound of killing miraculously transformed in his ears into the happy sound of a Saint Stephen's Day fireworks. He hobbled to the door to shout with the others milling around the bent tracks, burned-out railway cars, and the patched-up skeleton of the station. People on their way home: Polish and Ukrainian girls who had grown into womanhood in labor camps; Jews, the skin-and-bone remnants of Auschwitz and Belsen; Hungarian men and women dislodged by war; and soldiers. Victors and vanquished, they all shouted and cried and kissed each other. Peter, standing in the doorway of the boxcar looking at them, felt love rising in him for all the people, his brothers and sisters, spared by the mercy of God so that they all could live in peace. The mementoes of the war were still there, but he had already stepped over the threshold where war, hate, and fear were left behind like bad dreams in the morning.

"I am hungry," Sarah said. The firing of tommy guns tapered off.

"So am I," Peter said. "Let's go home."

She helped him down and they joined the throng of people scurrying about like rats or sitting on their bundles, with infinite patience waiting for a train or the news of one that would take them home. A woman stepped in front of Peter, carrying a small photograph like a sick bird in the palm of her left hand.

"Have you seen him? He is my son."

"No, but don't worry, the war is over now."

The woman left without a word, her eyes already scanning the crowd for returned soldiers.

"Can you walk on?" Sarah asked. Peter was watching the woman stop another soldier. The soldier shook his head.

"Of course I can," Peter said. They walked across what had been the platform.

"I feel dizzy," the girl said, walking slowly beside him.

"We'll eat soon. It's the sun on an empty stomach."

"Water would help. You know when one drinks very slowly, pretending. . . ."

"Yes," Peter said, seeing for the first time the armed Russian soldiers around the station. They were not waiting for a train to take them home. "The war is over," he murmured.

"What?"

"The war is over," he said, noticing the blue visor caps of the NKVD and the torn uniforms of the Hungarian soldiers herded in one corner of the station.

"Peter," the girl said. "Peter."

"I see Them," he said.

"Stoy!" the command came. "Halt."

"We are almost home," Peter said, going on; then he stopped. He heard the click of a rifle bolt. Two Russian soldiers in clean, neat uniforms, holding their rifles under their arms like hunters, converged on them. The smaller one grabbed Sarah by her arm and pointing with his head outside the station said, "Davay, davay." The girl just stood there looking up at Peter.

"Davay! Davay!"

"He wants you to go home," Peter said.

"I have no place to go," she said; then, when the other soldier stamped the ground with his feet, she began to run. She ran like a stray dog, with her head turned back every third or fourth step to look at Peter. Once she stopped altogether, but the soldier again stamped the ground and she went on running, her ankles buckling under her as she stepped on pieces of brick and cement. Finally she was out of sight, lost among the rubble. The soldiers laughed and good-naturedly nudged Peter to join the prisoners in one corner of the railway station. There were twenty-five of them from all branches of the Hungarian Army, a dirty, dejected lot, some of them without shoes, sitting or standing in little groups. As Peter hobbled closer to them, a horse-faced artilleryman jumped up from the ground where he was sitting and rushed at him.

"This is an officer," he screamed. "Take him. I am a proletarian. I want to go home." He spat at Peter. "See him standing here high and mighty? I am a proletarian, I tell you."

Two men pulled him away and sat him down on the ground again. An NKVD officer walked up to Peter now.

"Do you speak German?" he asked, addressing him in German.

"Yes, I do."

"Where did you learn to speak German?"

"As a child I had a German nanny." The NKVD officer was now standing almost nose to nose with Peter. "You are lying."

"I am not lying."

"So you are not lying. It was the German nanny who told you to pretend that you are wounded?"

Peter didn't answer.

"Drop your crutch!"

The crutch fell with a clatter on the pockmarked asphalt platform.

"Walk!"

"I can't walk."

"Where are you wounded?"

"Here." Peter pointed at his right thigh where his riding breeches were slit to allow for the thick, dirty bandages.

"We'll see," the NKVD officer said and gave an order in Russian. Two of his soldiers came to stand on each side of Peter. "Walk!"

"I can't without the crutch."

"No?" He shouted something in Russian.

Peter heard a horrible, animal-like sound; then his head hit the platform. He didn't feel pain. He knew only that some warm liquid was slowly coursing down into his boot and remembered his father telling him that a gentleman always tries to avoid creating a scene and opened his eyes. It was blood. He felt a sense of relief; then his thigh started to throb with agonizing, tearing pain. Somebody gently kicked his good leg. A Russian soldier was bending over him.

"Davay," he said. Peter was pulled up and the crutch thrust under his right armpit. Standing once more, he saw the NKVD officer unconcernedly smoking a cigarette and the prisoners huddled together like cattle in the wind. He wondered if he should not walk up to the NKVD officer and do something that would build up the men's morale, but a new dizziness made him forget the men and his duty. All he knew was that the crazy angle of the sky was threatening him somehow and that pain which had been contained in the sector of his right thigh burst through and took over the whole of his body.

"Davay," the Russian soldier said kindly, his outstretched arm pointing the direction. Peter went slowly, trying to keep the sky, now blindingly white and dotted with sharp, black dots, from turning over and pushing him down into the blackness of the ground. Concentrating hard, he hobbled on; one, two, one, two, his left boot kicking away broken bits of brick, one, two, his crutch writing a monotonous Morse code: one, two. He passed the line of armed Russian soldiers ringing the railway station and was among mountains of brick, splintered wood, and chunks of mortar. Crushed houses which had become hills with ridges and valleys and slopes, houses turned into burial vaults smelling of the sweet smell of death. The footpath opened into a street where houses stood, some listing, some shored up but standing. He hobbled on a sidewalk, noticing empty, glassless shopwindows where women and a few old men sat, two or three to a shopwindow, selling their wares. They looked at him with frightened eyes, in silence. One, two, one, two. There were other pedestrians on the sidewalk. Not running or crouching in doorways but walking. He had come home. One, two. . . .

"Good, fresh hard rolls," somebody called out. Peter stopped, dragging his crutch upright. The woman was sitting in the shopwindow, next to a laundry basket full of hard rolls. Hard rolls used to be served for breakfast on white plates, sliced in two, ready for butter and jam.

"I didn't mean to," he croaked.

"It's all right," the woman said. Peter jammed the hard roll into his mouth and went on. One, two, one, two. The shopwindows and the people in them were weaving from side to side. Tick, tock, tick, tock. There was a grandfather clock in the dining room. The pendulum swung between ivory columns. One, two, tick, tock. He felt the dizziness coming again. Where was he? Where was home in this disfigured, bashed-in, strange city? It used to be a long way from the railway station, suitcases cramping his legs as the cab drove past three bridges, then turned left by the monastery with its many sweet bells, and crept up a steep hill to a quiet, tree-lined street. There were no taxicabs, not even streetcars. One, two, one, two. A building was missing here, then shopwindows again and people in them. Tick, tock, tick, tock. An old man wanted to give him a cigarette, but Peter couldn't stop now. The house was far away and the sun got brighter and brighter. The black dots were coming back, making his heart race madly. One, two, one, two.

He was standing in front of a shopwindow seeing the glinting, jagged edge of glass in the black-burned frame. The dusty wooden floor was partly covered with a sheet of brown paper. A woman was sitting on it with a basket on her lap. There were cornmeal cookies in her basket. Bright yellow, he could see that clearly. The woman was wearing a calico dirndl as if dressed for a costume ball. There was something wrong with her. They were looking at each other. Her eyes were brown and shaped like his own and she was crying, sitting there with the basket on her lap. Then she lifted her arms.

"I won't be able to get up, Mother," Peter said, sitting on the brown paper beside her, not hearing her say "My son," and explaining that she had been waiting here every day for the past three months, knowing that he must come this way because she had prayed. He couldn't hear anything. His ears were filled with the noise of eating the bright yellow cookies.

Pictures in a Cigar Box

At the age of nine he wanted to lead a cavalry charge followed by his troop of hussars with drawn swords, dressed in blue dolmans with gold braid on their shoulders, gold frog fasteners on their chests and red britches tucked into black, shiny boots, exactly what his own father was wearing in the hand-colored photograph that he had found among the discards in a cigar box, even though his Uncle Miklos had told him that the last cavalry charge of World War I was made in 1915 with disastrous consequences. Uncle Miklos knew it firsthand. He had been commanding a squadron of hussars of the Austro-Hungarian Imperial Army. Thereafter, according to his father, Uncle Miklos decided not to become a hero and had wangled an assignment to buy replacement horses for the cavalry in Sweden. (There were several pictures of Swedish lakes and naked ladies in the cigar box. Uncle Miklos had explained to him that Swedish ladies didn't wear bathing costumes.) But, unlike Uncle Miklos, he wanted to be a war hero. In his imagination he always died in the charge, dying a heroic death followed by a glorious military funeral with the open coffin resting on a caisson pulled by four Lipizzaners. The only thing that defeated his imagination was the absence of the regulation hussar mustache on his upper lip.

At fifteen he wanted to suffer martyrdom for his faith. He and his friend Tibor were the only Protestants among forty-two boys in class

5-A of their gymnasium. It was a Piarist school, taught by the *patres scholarum piarum,* famous for demanding high standards from their pupils. His mother had enrolled him over the protestations of his paternal grandparents, who complained that religion was as much a part of the curriculum as was Latin, mathematics, or art. An agreement was reached: while the rest of 5-A had religious instruction, he and Tibor went into the courtyard to fly paper airplanes folded to Tibor's design that could in the spring reach the stratospheric heights of the open schoolroom windows.

The two of them attended religious instruction classes with the other Protestant boys of the district twice a week after school. Protestant church history was taught by their regular dominie, who also demanded that they turn in abstracts — one page in length, written in neat hand — of his Sunday sermons as proof of their attention at church services. Dominie Losonczy, whose hero, Oliver Cromwell the Lord Protector, was held up to be emulated by them, went so far as to rate the Roundhead soldiers above even the Hungarian hussars. The boys sniggered when they heard the dominie say this or warn them that they were only a step away from perdition, living as they were in a sea of Roman Catholicism. This always made him anxious, even though only Tibor knew (and was sworn to secrecy) that his own mother was a Roman Catholic. What even Tibor didn't know was that his mother quite often took him to Mass and that when the priest dismissed them with the *ite, missa est,* he felt light and clean even without the sacraments that were forbidden to him. Most of the time his mother took him to what was colloquially known as the "Printers' Mass" early in the morning before the household awoke. They never met anybody they knew. The few half-asleep communicants were total strangers. He had heard so many times that the Calvinists were thicknecked that he actually believed he was visibly different from the majority of his Roman Catholic countrymen, as if he had been marked with an indelible bar sinister. He had never asked his mother how she felt about it but took it for granted that he was an embarrassment to

45

her, even though sometimes she asked him to accompany her to High Mass to hear Mozart's *Requiem* or Beethoven's *Missa Solemnis*.

His longing for martyrdom was precipitated by his feeling of guilt for going to Mass with his mother that coincided with Dominie Losonczy's lecture on the murder of the Huguenots on St. Bartholomew's Eve, August 23, 1572. This was no dry history lecture. They were given the gory details as if the massacre had been perpetrated the day before, on Tuesday (religion classes were always on Wednesdays and Fridays), where Protestant boys and girls were split in two, where mothers on their knees begging for the lives of their little ones were run through with pikes, where dignified old Huguenots looking like their own grandfathers and grandmothers were used for épée practice. His pain and guilt were exacerbated by the fact that his own grandfather on his mother's side, the beloved one with the shaved head and curled moustache who walked around as if he had swallowed an ironing board, was French, a Roman Catholic, and a one-time épée champion at Saint-Cyr.

On Thursday morning between trigonometry and Latin, he fought a boy, at least a year and a half older, from 6-B. He did not achieve martyrdom, perhaps because he had used brass knuckles and the boy had cried, and that made him feel even more guilty, knowing full well that his own father believed that using brass knuckles was a cowardly thing that no gentleman would ever think of doing. The brass knuckles belonged to their chauffeur, who definitely was not a gentleman. He had seen him steal neckties from his father's wardrobe.

That same afternoon he fought another boy, almost nineteen, from class 8-A. This time it was Fr. de Cossell, his French literature teacher, who put the possibility of a martyr's crown out of reach by taking him to his office. He could always talk with Fr. de Cossell because his Hungarian had the same French accent as his mother's. Besides, some things were easier said in French.

"And nobody wanted to kill the Protestant. Nobody wanted to play the part of Catherine de Médicis, is that it?"

"Yes, Father."

"So there was no expiation for his sin of going to Mass with his mother. Of *liking* to go to Mass with his mother. Is that it?"

"Yes, Father."

"You must know that your father, your mother, and your French grandfather all love you."

Fr. de Cossell was acquainted with his mother and father and when he was in France had even visited his grandfather at La Galane, near Nice, and had stayed in his strangely shaped, lovely house that used to be an olive press.

"Yes, Father."

It had crossed his mind that the R.C.s may have something in the confessional: his burden had been lifted when for a whole year he had felt like Atlas supporting an impossible family constellation. "Impossible" had been his grandfather's word. He had overheard him talking with his mother when they were visiting him over the Christmas holidays. At home, at their village, everybody belonged to the Reformed Church because the peasants had followed his father's family in the eighteenth-century Reformation. He had no right to leave them. He, his father's son, was their icon, an icon that his mother's church, whose liturgy he loved because it made the region beyond the spatiotemporal visible to him, considered a bastard.

"Do you think I'm a bastard, Father? An illegitimate?"

"No, my son. You are a child of God. Nothing can be better than that."

*   *   *

On his twenty-third birthday, the twenty-sixth of February 1946, he hijacked a Red Army truck loaded with food. It was the coldest winter in memory. The heavens above had not rained down righteousness, only snow. The remaining trees of Budapest's many parks — those that had not been cut down by artillery fire, aerial bombardments, soldiers of the opposing armies, or by the civilian remnant — were shattered by the cold. The truck was a lend-lease Studebaker. He thought it was of Soviet manufacture because the instructions on the base of the gear-shift lever were written in Cyrillic letters. Not that it really mattered. He had figured out the shifting pattern fast enough to get away with the load of bread and lard. Though there was official peace now, people still died from starvation, gunshot wounds, and the cold. His sister, who lived on the Buda side in the cellar of their collapsed villa, was in constant fear of not being able to feed her baby. Her husband, a brain surgeon, worked at a clinic on the Pest side. He was housed and fed there. Budapest's five bridges had been blown up by the retreating Germans. There was now only one temporary pontoon bridge across the Danube.

The stealing of the Studebaker truck was a spontaneous act, not something that he had planned to do. He had gone to see his sister and his baby niece as a birthday gift to himself. The path leading to the cellar door was only partly cleaned of the broken brick and mortar of the collapsed house to disguise the fact that people lived there. He knocked on the door with his fist, then listened to the silence. Nothing moved inside.

"It's me, Evike. It's Karcsi." He heard furniture dragged back; then the door opened and his sister was standing there, her pale face pock-marked with red lipstick dots to mimic some dread venereal disease, her only defense against being raped again.

"I have no more milk," she said. "I can't nurse Lucy anymore."

*   *   *

The Blue Marble restaurant down behind the charred Royal Palace on Castle Hill, which had been the Germans' last stand in Budapest, had somehow survived with only its plate glass windows blown out. Though boarded over, it was open for customers who either had saved up their food coupons, bought them on the black market, or paid the exorbitant prices for dishes made of lungs and other offal. The olive-drab Studebaker truck loaded with round loaves, the crust the color of dark leather, was parked at the curb in front of it. Against the cab wall, looking like chimney bricks, frozen one-kilo lard packages were piled, blocking the back window. There was nobody in the cab. The soldiers must have gone into the restaurant to transact their own black market deal. There was a Red Army winter cap on the seat and a submachine gun, its round magazine the color of pewter where the blueing had rubbed off. He opened the door on the driver's side. The sound of metal scraping on metal made people on the sidewalk look toward the truck. He turned the ignition key, jammed the Red Army winter cap on his head, and shifted into gear.

*   *   *

He traded some of the bread and lard for fresh milk, powdered milk, cornmeal, beans, winter apples, and pumpkins. The rest he gave away.

He enjoyed playing Robin Hood against a regime that had not only betrayed the downtrodden of the world in the name of the downtrodden of the world but had also taught them to become liars. Party lines were parroted like magical mantras to keep away the KGB, AVO, STASI, or whatever the midnight visitors were called. Sometimes the mantras were reinforced with money in the hope of sharing space — one room and the use of the kitchen — in an apartment that more often than not had once been the petitioner's own. With no housing, people could not keep their jobs, and the government relocated them and their families to where they were most needed — to the coal mines or to the newly organized collective farms that were called, euphemistically, "co-ops." Never mind that the workers' training was in the humanities, law, philosophy, or the arts.

This relocation order was a virtual death sentence for city people over sixty. They were taken to outlying villages to live in drafty barns while trying to transform themselves from parasites into useful farm

laborers. It usually took only one winter for the final relocation to oc-
cur.

After a while the most inane slogans had become part of people's
lives, with the attendant suspicion and paranoia. He had no male
friends left with whom he could talk beyond soccer, women, dead
schoolmates, or news of the availability of some food item. He had to
be careful even with Tibor because the woman he lived with was the
local party secretary of the quarry workers. Even the Church had
changed. Not the words used in the services but the way those words
were conveyed and emphasized to give them a safe Marxist tinge, as if a
demented Paracelsus had succeeded in turning gold into lead to change
the messianic hope into a deadly communist utopia.

He had changed too. In his relatively short life he had been taught
time and time again to number his days. He had survived the fighting
on the Eastern Front and the long retreat from Kiev. His heart was
aware that only his own death, the sought-after destiny, would bring
real peace. He had read about Gulliver's horrific encounter with the
Struldbruggs, who were condemned to live on and on into infinity; of
Baron Munchausen, doomed to the same fate. He had read both books
at an early age. Even then he had understood enough about the de-
pressing nature of a never-ending life in a changing world to reject it.
After the cataclysm of World War II it was easier for him to bury God
under the millions of decaying corpses than to accept the idea of free
will that implicated him in the enormity of the sin and guilt of his gen-
eration. But forsaking God did not break his yoke. Instead of freedom,
he had felt the bitterness of one tied even more to the blood-drenched
earth he had wanted to escape.

After the first stolen truck he never played Robin Hood again, perhaps because about the same time he was offered a job by Herr Diamant,
a family acquaintance. Herr Diamant summoned him to Gundel's, one of
Budapest's finest restaurants, whose internationally famous cuisine had
survived two world wars. He knew Gundel's from his boyhood — the fes-
tive *déjeuner* provided by his visiting grandfather when he was seven to cel-

ebrate the end of his scarlet fever quarantine — and when he was older, the many eleven o'clock light lunches with his father. Nowadays only the most successful black marketeers could afford to patronize Gundel's. Herr Diamant, who had holdings in both Austria and Hungary, had fled the Nazis after the "Anschluss" to seek refuge in Hungary. He remembered Herr Diamant only vaguely as a family acquaintance who unpredictably shuttled between their family farms and summer houses. When he was home on leave from the Eastern Front, he had provided the transportation for Herr Diamant. He was always told to wear his uniform on those occasions and to play the young staff officer too important to stop at roadblocks because Herr Diamant's identification papers were of questionable quality. Now, going to Gundel's in the threadbare uniform that constituted his entire wardrobe, he felt self-conscious. He had borrowed an unlined Burberry overcoat to cover up his botched attempt at dyeing the khaki uniform jacket black. The overcoat was too small. The porter at the entrance halted him and sent an apprentice to fetch the headwaiter.

"Yes?" The headwaiter, a graying, slim man in striped trousers and frock coat, could have been a stand-in for a member of parliament in Dickens's time. "Yes? May I help you?"

The headwaiter's tone of voice instantly transformed him into Gundel's persona non grata. It was warm in the foyer and he could smell the "Wild Board Gourmet Style." As a boy he would go with his father to hunt wild boar to be served with green peppers, tomatoes, mushrooms, parsley, potato croquettes, smoked tongue flavored with bay leaf and peppercorn with red wine, paprika, red currant jelly, thyme, and juniper berries. It took two days for Cook to prepare the Wild Board, and she always insisted on extra help.

Wild boars with their curved tusks had terrified him, but he would not hurt his father by revealing his own cowardly self. People still talked about his Great Uncle Mihaly, who was ripped open by a wild boar. When he was big enough to aim the 9-millimeter Mannlicher, he stopped being afraid and began to think of himself as his father's squire, ready to give his life for his knight.

"I'm here to see Herr Diamant. He's expecting me."

"Of course, sir," the headwaiter said ingratiatingly. "Sorry to have kept you waiting. The boy garbled the message." With one smooth move of his hand he cuffed the apprentice. "Please follow me."

He tipped the headwaiter with the last of his money and followed him thinking that some things, like the kilometer stones by the side of the roads, remained unchanged whatever the regime.

"Charles, my dear friend," Herr Diamant shouted from his table. He spoke in Viennese-accented Hungarian that the natives found charming. Very few of the foreigners spoke Hungarian. Those who did were revered. During the war, the BBC's Hungarian language service had employed an Englishman, a college professor, as a news reader. Hungarians, who would have questioned the veracity of another Hungarian living in London, tended to believe the professor simply because of his English accent. "Come and sit down."

"Thank you." He had been baptized "Karoly." To his friends he was "Karcsi." Only his mother and his relatives on her side called him "Charles." He hated it. "Charles" sounded affected in Hungarian. There were two men and three women sitting around the table. The women were beautiful in the sexually explicit way of the movie queens whose pictures he had seen in old Hollywood fan magazines. "Demimonde" his mother would have called them in a tone of voice reserved for Germans and people with vulgar tastes. He would have given his soul for their friendship.

"Take the lieutenant's coat." Herr Diamant snapped his fingers.

Two waiters rushed to his side and removed the borrowed Burberry to reveal his dirty-green tunic, the result of his botched attempt with black dye.

"I insist you tell me the name of your tailor, Charles," Herr Diamant said.

"Latza is such a card," one of the women laughed. She had lipstick on her teeth. They all laughed. He tried to laugh with them but blushed instead. Herr Diamant, who couldn't be more than a few years older than himself, was sitting there surrounded by adoring young women in tight silk blouses that he wanted to touch even more than he wanted to eat the potato croquettes and the slice of wild boar on Herr Diamant's plate.

"Bring a menu for the lieutenant." Latza was clicking his fingers again. The headwaiter himself brought the menu and, bending down, held it in front of him, slowly turning the pages as if it were sheet music.

"No, thank you," he said, waving the headwaiter and the menu away, trying to keep his saliva safely inside his mouth.

"How about a taste, Charles?" Latza was pushing his plate over to him.

It was a question of character. He didn't have any. He ate all that remained on Latza's plate, and because he knew how to use explosives, he was hired to interdict Red Army food shipments. His "honorarium" (like "interdict," it was Latza's word) would be food for his mother and sister and for him bed and board at Erzsebet's. Erzsebet was the young woman with the lipstick-smeared teeth. Latza was to supply the inside information and to dispose of the intake from the food convoys. "Intake" and "dispose" were also Latza's words, as was "termination": "The occasional termination of non-targeted trucks and personnel could be necessitated by the orderly execution of the operation."

On that day at the end of February he had to acknowledge for the first time since leaving the gymnasium that his teachers, the *patres scholarum piarum*, were right in teaching subjects that he had thought irrelevant for the twentieth century. He remembered reading Pascal, who had noted in the seventeenth century the "insincerity with which terms are carefully chosen to cover opposite meanings."

*   *   *

Erzsebet's apartment was just off Vaci Street, Budapest's "Fifth Avenue," where the most elegant and expensive shops had been located before the siege. Five months of fighting had burned out most of the shops, and those that were not destroyed were looted by the contending armies. Vaci Street ran parallel to the Danube and the great hotels on the eastern bank of the river with their boarded-up windows and bullet-hole-peppered facades facing toward the hills of Buda, the burned-out Royal Palace on Castle Hill, the miraculously intact Matthias Church with its colorful tile roof, and the white stones of the Fishermen's Bastion. Erzsebet's apartment house had two entrances that were easy to observe from her windows, and there was always a crowd on the streets as if to make up for the months of curfew: workmen carting away rubble, shoring up sagging houses, and even installing glass in some of the hotel windows. There was a thriving black market twenty-four hours a day in foreign currency, Napoleon gold pieces, gold bullion, silver, Leica cameras, antiques, jewelry, paintings (some stolen from art museums, some from deportees' houses and apartments). Almost anything could be bought with U.S. dollars and gold.

Erzsebet's apartment was safe, if anything could be called safe in a black market operation conducted under the nose of an ever-tightening Red Army occupation, and was in fact Latza's office. Occasionally, families or unconnected individuals stayed in the apartment in transit to the West and freedom. These were lucrative business transactions, since Latza could show that the risks and the bribes were high. There were messengers coming and going, couriers bringing cigarette paper, flint, penicillin stolen from the U.S. Army in Austria, nylon stockings from Italy, sewing machine needles from Germany, and fine wines from all over Europe. It was in the apartment that he had met Nikita, the Ukrainian nationalist who got a percentage of Latza's take because he knew Red Army (just lately renamed "Soviet Army") regulations and procedures. He had been one of them before going AWOL. Nikita used the money to buy ammunition and guns for his brethren still fighting Stalin in the Ukrainian forests. He and Nikita had become partners in the "interdictions." The first three weeks netted, on the average, three Soviet Army food trucks a day. Latza's intelligence was right on target.

They knew exactly where the driver and his helper took their breaks. There was no need to blow ditches in the highways. The civilians on the streets were unreliable witnesses. They never looked at Soviet Army soldiers. They hated them all. Wearing a Red Army uniform was a small price to pay for the smoothness of the operation.

At first, action brought on paralyzing fear that he fought with his old, tried system of turning himself into a zombie who without conscious thought would click off the safety on his stolen Russian automatic, open the door of the truck designated to be stolen, look at the ignition (the key was usually left in), scan the street, check Nikita covering him from a doorway, lay the automatic on the seat beside him, put the truck in gear, start, stop, pick up Nikita, drive again with the muscles in his back so tight that he could hardly breathe, turn at the first corner and the next, and the next again. When Nikita said it was safe to stop, he would open the cab door and vomit on the pavement. After a while he didn't need to become an automaton. He became addicted to the high of the pumping adrenaline and the close comradeship that sprung up between people in war. He and Nikita had become brothers. They both knew that it was only a question of time before they would die. Safety was never an absolute. Patrols could come at any time. It was the war all over again except that torture was now an expected fate before dying.

*   *   *

It had come as a shock to him that Erzsebet, the object of his lust, seldom lunched at Gundel's, never used makeup, and had been taught by the nuns so well that her Latin was better than his own. He found out that she was alone in the world because her brother, who had been a captain of infantry, had died on the banks of the Dnieper, and her grandmother, who had brought them up — both of their parents had died in a car accident — was also dead. The biggest shock of all was the realization that his lust had turned into love. They would walk down

55

Vaci Street among the burned-out stores where people sat in the display windows bundled up against the cold, selling cigarettes, silver candelabra, pumpkins, opera glasses, whalebone corsets, meerschaum pipes, anything that might be traded for beans, potatoes, lard, or a bit of oil, the minimal necessities of life. The sellers were a pinched-faced, hungry lot, yet they smiled at their obvious love that somehow brought hope even among the ruins that hate had created and was creating still.

One day they walked further than usual, passing the rubble of Vörösmarty Square, the burned-out cars, a Russian tank with its cannon pointing down like the trunk of an elephant, the shattered walls of Gerbeaud's famous pastry shop, another tank, this time a German one, houses where the front walls were missing but the rooms with their furniture and paintings remained intact, reminding Erzsebet of the inside of the doll's house her grandmother had given her on her tenth birthday. She was crying and put their joined hands in his coat pocket. He had a real coat now with fur lining.

They had come to what was left of the Chain Bridge. The suspension part of the bridge was submerged in the Danube, which was not blue but a ghastly greenish color. They were standing there freezing in the wind, looking across to Buda, which was again a separate city where, flanking the wharf, chimneys stood like tombstones marking the places where people had lived.

"Stay with me, please," he said.

"I will. Always." She squeezed his hand.

*   *   *

He didn't like leaving Erzsebet behind unprotected. Latza's business operation had a dark underside which seemed embodied in the two women, Ildiko and Mitzi, whom he had first met at Gundel's sitting at the table with Latza, Erzsebet, and the two men. Ildiko and Mitzi would sometimes stay at Erzsebet's apartment overnight with men

Latza designated as "important clients." If he was not on an operation or was lying low afterward to protect their HQ, he and Erzsebet acted as hosts, a role he despised because he had to watch Erzsebet with the guests, glitteringly clever in her little girl's way.

The "interdiction" operation had temporarily moved a hundred miles outside Budapest toward Szeged, where a safety-match factory was producing for the Soviet Army. Matches had become for a time the premium trade goods. Since matches were shipped in convoys, he had begun blowing up highways. The most important first step — Latza supplied the convoys' route — was to select the ambush site, where the explosives were placed with their percussion caps one-and-a-half meters apart in their almost invisible cylindrical nests. The one wired explosive that would set off the rest was ignited with electricity supplied by a bicycle dynamo. The six extra drivers, Volga Tartars, did the rest. Three weeks later, when he was back in Budapest with Erzsebet, he first heard about Joran. Joran was a Swedish businessman who had come to Budapest to do business with the Communists — his country had done business with the Nazis, supplying all their ball bearing needs during the war — but ended up instead with Latza in the more lucrative black market. Joran's charmingly accented German redeemed the language which had become synonymous with Hitler's ranting. He had met him with Erzsebet over lunch at Gundel's.

They left Joran at the restaurant and walked to the corner of Vaci Street and the short tunnel that led to the Danube. It began to snow. Just inside the tunnel on the sidewalk a woman was roasting chestnuts on top of a steel barrel heated to a deep red color from the burning charcoal. The woman, another barrel of coats and scarves, wearing gloves that exposed the ends of her fingers, was filling newspaper funnels with chestnuts.

"Get two for the mistress. One for each pocket," she said. "It'll warm her hands and she will be true to you forever."

"Four each, please," he said, looking at Erzsebet, at the sharp planes of her face under a new fur hat. The snowflakes on her eyelashes made him think of family Christmases when he was still safe and secure.

He paid the woman, and they walked through the tunnel where they could look across the Danube at Buda. Once more the falling snow transformed the ruins into fairy-tale crystal palaces, making it possible for them to forget that only six months ago the tunnel behind them had been used as a holding pen for people who were later marched down to the river to be shot.

"You have a new fur hat," he said.

"Yes. . . . What are you trying to do?"

"Look into your eyes."

"You want to look into my head."

"Yes." The wind rose, lifting the curtain of snow, revealing the forlorn chimneys and the pitiful ruins frozen into a landscape where hope was already dead. She was standing close to him, her hand in his coat pocket holding his. They were like lost children, Hansel and Gretel in dark woods not of their own making.

"I love Joran but not the way I love you."

"And you went to bed with him." They were still holding hands. "Why?" He was whispering as if not hearing his own question could make it moot. "Why?"

"I don't know if you'll be alive tomorrow. I don't know if we can ever live together like normal people. Can you understand? Joran wants to take me to Sweden. . . . I want to live in a place that's safe, not in an apartment that the police or the AVO might raid at any moment. I don't want to end up in a concentration camp."

It helped that the snow was coming down harder, turning him into a snowman. Snowmen did not feel because they had no blood in their veins and they had the advantage that when spring came they melted away.

"Why are you still holding my hand?" he said.

"Did they read you the 'Pooh' stories when you were little?"

"Yes," he said.

"There's one where Piglet comes up to Pooh and takes Pooh's paw and just holds it, and when Pooh asks him what he wants he says, 'Nothing. I just wanted to be sure of you.' Do you remember it?"

"I wish it was spring already," he said.

*   *   *

The next operation took him away from Budapest again. There were no loaded single army trucks on the streets or highways anymore. Latza thought it was almost time to halt these operations altogether. There was one more planned, the grandfather of them all, which involved the re-hijacking of six American Army trucks that had been taken by a high-ranking Soviet officer, a relative of Voroshilov, in a quasi-official, deniable operation. The six trucks were loaded with SPAM, which had kept the American Army moving in the war and was used now, in the U.S. sectors, as currency to pay for laundry, sex, wine, or anything else the American GIs couldn't find in their PXs.

Latza's intelligence reported that the hijacked convoy had moved into the Austrian sector of the Soviet Zone, then at Prellenkirchen to the Czech side of the Soviet Zone, then had crossed over to Soviet-occupied Hungary at Nyergesujfalu. For five days the convoy was hidden in the Visegrad Mountains at Dobogóko. On the sixth day Latza's inside contact phoned to say the convoy was on the move again.

The ambush was set in the bend of the river where the narrow highway was hemmed in on one side by the Danube and on the other by the Visegrad hills. It was a cold, sunny day without a breeze, which made the wide surface of the river look like dark-gray glass.

"After this I won't be seeing you much, Charles," Nikita said in German. They both spoke German. "Maybe never again."

They were standing by the roadside with a bicycle to turn the dynamo wired to an explosive to set off the rest of the charges with the effect of the percussion. The bicycle was also a prop. Who would notice two men working on a broken-down bike?

"I was eleven the first time I ever cycled more than five kilometers by myself. I was on this road. My family had a villa fifteen kilometers from here. They wouldn't buy me a dynamo, though, because they worried that if I had a headlight I would stay out at night."

"My family never had a dacha," Nikita said, "and they never worried about me. My old man tried to pickle himself in vodka, and my mother was worn out with work and standing in line to feed us. Only my babushka cared about me. She was a street cleaner. She died of pneumonia."

In the distance they could hear the convoy buzzing like a colony of angry bees. Nikita lifted the bike by its saddle.

"Squat down," Nikita said.

He squatted down, his hand on the right pedal, thinking that horses and bikes were always mounted from the left and that he had discovered their planned escape route around the ruins of Visegrad Castle seven years ago at the age of sixteen only because he had wanted to be alone with a woman twice his age.

"Now," Nikita shouted. "Now."

He spun the wheel. Hearing the explosions, he was up, running toward the trucks, firing his tommy gun high, trying not to damage anything, hearing Nikita, then the six Volga Tartars firing too. He made the two men in the first truck get out and lie on their stomachs with their arms stretched out. Within seconds the other men were on their stomachs too, looking like so many crosses lying on the highway where he had first cycled more than five kilometers by himself. Then something slapped the back of his head, and he felt blood trickling down into his shirt collar and heard his own screaming above the sound of gunfire. He wasn't screaming because of pain. He was screaming to stop the horrors that changed them from a band of brothers to something unspeakably loathsome. Nikita and the Volga Tartars were shooting the men in the backs of their heads.

*   *   *

"Leave him," somebody said in Russian.

"No. Head wounds always bleed a lot," Nikita said.

"We have the trucks. You are compromising the operation."

"Can you hear me, Charles?" Nikita shouted.

He was floating toward the blue sky and Erzsebet said, "Just wanted to be sure of you." He knew that he had to love her more now if he wanted to love her at all. It made him very tired.

*   *   *

"I need to get at all the fragments, Sister."

"Does it help if I focus the light with the mirror?"

"You are a marvel, Sister. . . . You do know that we can both die for helping my dear brother-in-law. The only thing we ever had in common was Tannhäuser. . . . Have we got anything for pain — anything that won't be missed by the administration?"

"Morphine. I stole it."

"I am shocked, Sister."

"So am I."

"You have blood on your wimple, Sister. Calvinist blood. He'll think you are Catherine de Médicis. Karcsi, can you hear me?"

*   *   *

There were two kerosene stoves flanking his mattress, but he could still see his breath in the morning when the light came into the clinic's half-empty coal cellar through the slit of a window below the sidewalk. Sister had stayed with him the first two days. She had given him soup and boiled pumpkin, and they had talked about her being the bride of Christ, which assured her that she would never be betrayed as most wives were, her mother among them. She prayed for him, for all people in need, then thanked God for allowing them to have dialogue with Him and began to sing the *Dies Irae* in a sweet, small voice.

On the third day nobody came down to the cellar. Through the haze of his pain it was evening before he realized that the kerosene stove was out and his face was freezing. He willed himself to sleep but woke up feeling his heart banging the cage of his chest. He vaguely remembered that he had not eaten since the day before. He dozed off, then woke again smelling the coal, and it was morning. He thought it was his fourth morning in the coal cellar. The bandage on his head made him itch and he had to get up to urinate. He urinated on the coal where he had urinated before. There was something reassuring in the routine that reminded him of the way their cows and horses always walked on the same path to get to the water hole. When it had rained a lot, the water conquered new territories, even surrounding some of the trees that didn't like to get their feet wet. He had to walk through water to get to his knotted swinging rope hanging from an oak tree. It felt good to walk barefoot on the wet sand. It always rained in September just before school started. He had to wear shoes in school. Because of his family he had to wear shoes, could not be a shepherd playing his flute or lying on his back to look at the night sky as the shepherds did when they saw the star of Bethlehem. Schools had roofs and dress codes and study periods.

"Karcsi, wake up. You must eat," Sister said. "I couldn't come to see you before. The Russians are here at the clinic. You'll have to leave."

She had brought him a Russian winter cap. The earflaps covered his bandages; his overcoat was so shabby that even the Soviet Army soldiers would not want it. He was led from the coal cellar through the sewer by Uncle Mishi, who had been his grandfather's coachman and was now a porter at the clinic.

"They might kill you for helping me, Uncle Mishi."

"Them Russkies are too stupid to catch me, young lord."

"Don't call me 'young lord,' Uncle Mishi."

"What shall I call you?"

"Karcsi."

He surfaced close to the great Calvinist church. Parts of the street were torn up and the cobblestones piled into defensive nests. Some of these abandoned bulwarks were stained with blood and littered with broken weapons. There were people on the street sitting on chairs close to their apartment house doors, trying to trade various goods for food. Whenever Soviet Army soldiers appeared, they scurried inside. Others shuffled over the broken sidewalk looking as though they had forgotten where they wanted to go. Some halfheartedly lifted their hands to show him a few cigarettes, but to most it was obvious that he was not a good prospect. He walked like a drunk. He wanted to stop, to lie down somewhere, anywhere, but like a plague carrier whose nearness would cause death, he could not.

He had reached the Pest bridgehead of Erzsebet Bridge, a jumble of twisted steel next to the famed Inner City Parish Church, where his mother had taken him to High Mass. It was here that he had first been engulfed by the *Missa Solemnis*. The patinated roofs of the twin towers rose intact toward the leaden sky. The side door was not locked. He entered, touched the holy water in the receptacle with the fingertips of his right hand as his mother had taught him, genuflected, and made the sign of the cross. When he stood up he noticed the shallow basket, the kind that usually held the millstone-sized bread of peasant families, full of rainbow-colored paper money whose lowest denomination was the 1,000-pengo bill. The cost of a half-ounce of cooking oil was 10 million pengos on Tuesday. By Thursday the price could have doubled. He looked at the worthless money that today, at this hour, would still allow him to buy a meal, and began to stuff his pockets, then the inside of his shirt, with the oblations of the pious. He knelt down, resting his forehead on the back of the pew in front of him, feeling the blood slowly dripping into his shirt, soaking the stolen money. The only light came from the ruby glow of the lamp shining out of the darkness beside the main altar, illuminating in the face of Christ the glory of God that had made victory over death a reality even among the ruins.

He began to cry, his tears mingling with his blood.

The Acceptable Time

"Thank you very much. . . . Much obliged," he said. He had heard the click of the lighter and had shut his eyes. He could still see the flames, orange and red that turned gold and blue, shooting higher and higher. He waited to hear the explosion, all the while pretending that receiving a light for his cigarette was a normal transaction. It wasn't. He wasn't normal either. Though his face had healed and his eyebrows and eyelashes had grown back — the war for Hungary had ended nine months ago, a month before the ending of World War II — something inside him had been damaged so that any open flame could reproduce the exploding tank over and over again.

"Your politeness is overwhelming," Comrade Boros said in his mock-educated voice. He was party secretary of the village of Miklos in western Hungary.

"One of my class failings which I am working hard to rectify." The party jargon delivered in the wrong accent was incongruous.

"But in moderation, please, Andre," Comrade Boros's wife said. "I don't want you to start spitting on my clean kitchen floor like some Russian."

"Never fear." In spite of himself, he looked down. It was an evenly laid, clean brick floor. He remembered it from other times when he had visited here, when this house belonged to the Szabos. In pre-communist times Mr. Szabo was called a big peasant. Now he was called a "kulak," the Russian word for "fist," which conferred on Mr. Szabo and his family the supposed crimes of a class of people long dead of starvation, bullets, and beatings. The Szabos's seventy-five acres had become part of a state farm.

"You shouldn't sound reactionary in public, Kati," Comrade Boros said.

"Andre isn't the public."

"I agree. Andre is your pet reactionary."

"'Reactionary' is a word with many connotations," he said, in an accent that was as damaging to him as if he had worn a monocle, "all of them dangerous to the bearer."

"Would you like to debate me, Andre?"

"Why don't you get the wine, Boros," Kati said. It was one of her mannerisms to call her husband by his surname.

Comrade Boros got the jug from the sideboard and poured wine into their glasses. Silently they toasted each other.

"Not bad," Comrade Boros said.

"Not bad at all," he lied, thinking that his Uncle Pali would have died rather than pronounce this thin, new wine acceptable. It wasn't easy for him to address Comrade Boros. In pre-communist times he would have addressed an older man of his own class by his given name with "dear Uncle" added even when there were no family ties, but Comrade Boros wasn't his own class, which meant he couldn't greet him with the Latin "servus," either, and if he had said "God give us," he was certain he would not have received "a good day" in return. He remembered an Austrian skiing holiday with his parents before the war. Going down to breakfast, he had greeted the chambermaid with the usual Austrian "Bless God." Instead of "Bless God," the maid had given him a withering look and "Heil Hitler" in return. It was then that he first realized that a war had already begun.

He had come to Miklos two weeks ago simply because there was very little to eat in Budapest after the five-month siege. He knew that his Uncle Pali was dead and that the manor house had been ransacked, first by the Russians, then by the villagers, but it would still provide a roof over his head. Even if he couldn't buy food or barter for the hidden stocks of beans, flour, and lard, he could find food somehow. He counted on his Uncle Pali's gypsies to help him. Before the war the gypsies always wintered at Miklos Manor, literally dug into the ground. Visiting his uncle on Christmas school holidays, he had played with the gypsy children, watching them slide bare-bottomed down the snowy hillside into their warm burrows. During the war, the gypsies, along with the Jews, were deported. The deportation of the gypsies was endorsed by a large segment of his countrymen, the general consensus being that the gypsies would steal anything that wasn't nailed down or stabled. Only his Uncle Pali had the quaint notion that from God flowed inalienable dignity to each person. Uncle Pali had been killed by a German unit assigned to the deportation proceedings. The Germans were assisted by some of the more restless elements in the village who had joined the Arrow Cross party and had become the leading lights of Miklos, playing crucial roles in land confiscations, in the rationing of food, clothing, and soap, and in determining the size of quotas to be filled by the farmers. They were gone now, and were either living in Germany — East and West — or had been killed by people not very different from themselves other than that they derived their power from the Russian Army. They all saw that there was no such thing as inalienable dignity, that even their memory could be sullied, but they also knew that the role of victim could be exchanged for that of victor, and that was all that counted in this world.

The returning gypsy remnant demonstrated this belief by spitting on his boots when he stopped to talk to them. The women spat; the men looked on. At first he thought they didn't recognize him, their playmate and friend, couldn't recognize his face with its tight skin, but they did. They cursed his name because he was alive, because he didn't die like his Uncle Pali. Only death would have made him acceptable. The villagers wouldn't accept him, either. When Uncle Pali was alive, they had always invited him in to visit; now they avoided him as if he had some dread disease. He carried silver in his saddlebag: three soup spoons, a tea box, a snuffbox, a christening cup, and a sixteenth-century silver-plated gold communion chalice, but none of the villagers would trade for food or even allow him to set foot in their warm kitchens. He kept on trying. He had to. This time it was Mrs. Juhasz's kitchen. Through the door he could see an enameled water bucket on a chair in the corner, an enameled cup beside it. There was a large loaf of bread on the table swaddled in unbleached cloth. Then Mrs. Juhasz slammed the door. He turned and began to walk toward the farmyard gate, looking at the frozen goose and chicken droppings, wondering where the geese and chickens were. It was the coldest winter in memory that cracked the trees the artillery and the aerial bombardments hadn't destroyed. The gate opened before he reached it. A woman, stepping on the brick walkway, came toward him. She was his sister's age or his own, somewhere in her mid-twenties, dressed in clothes a city lady would wear for country outings.

"Save yourself a nasty experience," he said to her. "Mrs. Juhasz has no lard, no flour, no beans. She is hoarding even her words."

"Do you always believe what people tell you?" Hers was an educated voice, out of place here but one that went very well with her clothing, her face, her hair, reminding him of the poet Jozsef Attila, who wrote that even the hair of the gentry grew differently from that of the proletariat. "Follow me," she ordered him over her shoulder. "My name is Kati Boros." She knocked once, then marched into Mrs. Juhasz's kitchen.

*　　*　　*

Comrade Boros put the wine jug back on the sideboard, then lit the wick of the kerosene lamp, trimmed it, and put the glass chimney back. A whiff of kerosene in the air made the kitchen seem more cozy and secure. Watching Comrade Boros light the lamp, he was thinking that because of this strange couple — Kati, well-educated, cultured, upper middle class, and Comrade Boros, who sounded as if he had been born Party Secretary, out of Lenin, baptized by Stalin, without ever having had a father, mother, brothers, and sisters, kith or kin, or even a childhood with memories — it was possible for him to eat. From the moment Kati had marched him back into Mrs. Juhasz's kitchen, the shunning was over, as if the Boros aura and power had inoculated him against the unmentionable and unmentioned relationship with Miklos Manor and Uncle Pali. Since meeting Kati, he had spent every afternoon and evening in the Party Secretary's kitchen — the whole village knew it — talking about books and poetry and plays.

"Boros thinks Pirandello is a reactionary, too," Kati said. "I always liked him. He allows you to make up your own mind. The first time I saw *Henry IV*, I was certain that the king was mad. The second time I was sure that he faked it. What do you think, Andre?"

"He faked it."

"It's a question of one's point of view," Kati said. "What is truth? There is no such thing as objective truth, truth in capitals."

There is, he thought, afraid to say it out loud, betraying God with his silence because he wanted the warm kitchen, the food and drink, but even more because he didn't want Kati to think him a relic of the past.

"It's time for me to say good night."

"Not in the middle of a good discussion, Andre," Kati said.

"I mustn't overstay my welcome."

"Before you go, Andre, I must ask you something," Comrade Boros said. "Why were you climbing over the gate of the Reformed Church? You were seen, Andre."

"Because it's chained and padlocked."

"Only till the secretariat for Religious Affairs has inventoried it. What were you doing there?"

"I wanted to see if the wood carvings were all right. They were carved in my grandfather's time by an artist from Transylvania."

"Were they all right?" Kati asked.

"Yes. There were six carvings of God's promise to Noah after the Flood."

"Get the key to the padlock, Boros. I want to see them."

"You are out of your mind, Kati. State Security wanted to pick up Andre two hours ago. I had quite a time stopping them from coming here. I don't want their trucks and epaulets scaring the village to death."

"What about Andre? What will happen to him?"

"I told them I'd deliver him tomorrow morning. Their new headquarters are at the Karolyi Palace."

"You don't have to worry, Andre. Boros is going with you."

"I trust you to be here by six o'clock," Comrade Boros said. "You are considered one of the villagers, Andre. If you run away, you know what will happen to the village, not to speak of us?"

He did know. First the converging trucks, then the searches that would turn into robbery and rape.

"I'll be here," he said.

*   *   *

"Can you handle the horse?" Comrade Boros asked.

"Yes." He led out the gray spotted gelding, small and round like a circus horse, and hitched it to the trap. The smell of the horse almost made him forget why he was here this early in the morning, a morning that was still dark night lit only by the snow on the ground. The phrase *Terra autem erat inanis et vacua* came to his mind, and he thought that Dr. Mezö, if he were still alive, would be proud of him, but that the Reverend Losonczy, if he were still alive, would have a fit of apoplexy. His pastor wouldn't have liked Genesis quoted in Latin; to him it would have smacked of Counter-Reformation.

There were so many deaths around him that it was impossible to shut them out of his mind, to make them disappear the way he could once make the world go away just by shutting his eyes. There was a time when he only had to close his eyes to make the sun shine even in winter and know with absolute certainty that God loved him, love that allowed him to talk to God about anything that popped into his head. That was before he started school, before he was taught about disrespect.

"Did you close the gate, Andre?"

"I did."

"Put the brace in?"

"Yes."

"Let's go, then."

There was almost no movement of air other than that caused by the trap, as if the world were waiting with him for something evil to happen, evil that had lived since Cain and Abel in all recorded history, an immutable natural law that he wanted to counter with Isaac Newton's question — "Why may not Nature change bodies into light, and light into bodies?" — with confidence, so that the millions in the Ukraine who, as a result of a deliberate policy decision, died of starvation, and the millions who died in gas ovens, and the millions who died on endless battlefields, and the millions who died in the towns and cities could form a gigantic lamp to light the way to peace.

He watched the horse's white breath fly back to mingle with his own and Comrade Boros's breath in creaturely unity. The wheels of the trap crunched the thin snow covering the road. It was the only sound anywhere for a while; then the wind picked up with a loud sigh and swirled the snow on the fields beside the road. He looked up and saw the bright morning star.

*   *   *

The sun rose from behind the hills, a fireball illuminating the skeleton trees that seemed infested with a large, black fungi-like growth; then there was an explosion of feathers, and the crows, a black threatening twister, rose higher and higher to become a huge question mark that swooped down again, flying across the road up the side of the hill to the crest where the cemetery began. There was a squat, ugly house in which picks and shovels were kept and where strangers were laid out before burial. The crows settled on it, row upon row of noisy birds in a strange ritual, greeting the sun.

"You can walk from here, Andre," Comrade Boros said, reining in the horse. "It's less than a kilometer. When you get to the cross, take the right fork. You can see the Karolyi Palace from there."

He got down and watched Comrade Boros turn the trap around. He watched until the trap disappeared, feeling the snow seeping into his boots. Somewhere a dog barked and was answered by other dogs. The crows dispersed.

His footprints followed him in the virgin snow like a many-legged mythical beast. He was tired with sleeplessness, tired with fear. His feet were completely wet now, and his shoulders felt as if he had been carrying a heavy yoke of iron, heated just enough to hurt but not to kill. Then he saw the crucifix Comrade Boros had given as a landmark, and stopped. Snow covered the upper part of the cross and the top of the head. The upturned face was distorted as if by the added pain of the cold, the arms reaching out to him in an embrace just halted by the nails. He stood there waiting for something to happen, as he had waited in the war for the food to catch up with them, or the bombardment to stop, waiting without thinking, waiting without really expecting the food to catch up or the bombardment to stop. Then without any preliminaries the waiting was over, and the acceptable time was now. He again knew with absolute certainty that God loved him, that the tomb was empty, that without the living God he would be deaf and blind, dead in fact, one of the walking dead who bravely waited in an existential darkness for the horror to strike again. It was as if everything in his life pointed to this intersection in the road, telling him to come forward, show himself, the schoolboy who without any pause had become the soldier, contaminated first by the horrors of war, then by the horrors of peace supervised by the state security apparat. Infused by the Power that could make even this day a day of salvation, he took the right fork in the road and saw the Karolyi Palace, the new State Security Police headquarters, as Comrade Boros had said he would. He saw the guards with their blue epaulets, and machine pistols across the front of their Russian uniforms. He knew that they were Hungarians from the way they looked at him; nobody hated Abel more than Cain. He marched toward them, not feeling the cold snow in his broken boots or the pain in his shoulders or the pain in his stomach that had lived there for years like a hungry rat gnawing through a packing case. He marched in the triumph of his God.

The Barbershop on Kärtner Strasse

Karolyi Palace's large kitchens were below ground level, the light coming in through grates set into the wall at ceiling height. The Hungarian State Security had converted the kitchens into small, irregular cells for their political prisoners. His own cell measured three by five meters and was furnished with a metal bed without a mattress, a gray blanket, and a bucket whose chemical smell had burned into the lining of his nose. Some of the space was taken up by a wide, unused, brick chimney that had given the illusion of warmth when he was first brought down in the winter. It was summer now. He had been up all night, unable to sleep, his thoughts touching nerve ends with the cruelty of a dentist's slow drill. He was young enough — twenty-three — to remember his parents', nanny's, and even his tutor's hugs after punishment for one of his misdoings (he was the eleven-year-old boy who had kicked a tennis ball through the window of the parliament building in Budapest while parliament was in session), so that he had still expected forgiveness or at least mercy when his torture started. Since he had been in prison, he seemed to have reverted to that time in his life when he believed that love was more important than riches, security, education, or anything else, and that God would intervene to stop evil in the world. He hadn't slept all night because yesterday morning, for the first time since winter, he had not been taken to the interrogation rooms to be hog-tied or beaten, and he knew that after the interrogations stopped the executions always came on the following Saturday. He would have kept on denying this knowledge had he not seen a newspaper headline announcing that Comrade Gero was coming to inspect the Karolyi facility on August 15. That was all he had time to read before the guard finished with the sports section and turned to the front page after punching him in the face. Prisoners were not allowed to look at newspapers. Once when he was on a work detail he had looked through the open window of a guard's olive-green Trabant to read the folded newspaper left on the front seat. For reading "U.N. Demands" he was hog-tied for so long that the prison doctor made them cut the ropes. He never found out what the U.N. demanded.

Whenever possible, executions were always timed to coincide with the visits of Comrade Gero, the government minister who not only enjoyed hangings but would also, on occasion, put on a long butcher's apron and shoot kneeling prisoners in the back of the head.

Light was seeping through the grates. The sun was rising. He didn't know what day it was. He didn't know how many days he had left. He didn't know why God had abandoned him.

*   *   *

On his first day in prison he had been given potato soup with sausage and a thick slice of black bread and was allowed to sit next to a stove to dry out his boots. In the office he was given cigarettes, then was asked why he had come to the Bakony part of Hungary and if he had seen the Soviet military installations scattered in the mountains. He had not seen the military installations. He had come because people were starving in Budapest and there was always more food in the villages. He used to have an uncle living around here. They knew all about his uncle. Did he think the Communists were stupid, that they couldn't provide food for the people? He didn't say that. But he thought that, wasn't that the truth? Or was he spying for the Americans? He only knew Americans from books and the movies.

He was taken down to his cell. The next day, in the evening, two guards came to escort him — it was the last time he thought of it in terms of being escorted — through long underground passages to a peeling, brown door.

"You go in first," the older guard with the bored face told the younger one.

"Why should I go first?"

"Because I am telling you. Piros likes you."

"To hell with Piros." But he opened the thick brown door. "Hey, Piros. We've brought you a patient."

"You don't have to shout. I don't like noisy people." Piros stood just beyond the open door. "You've brought me a real tall one."

"About five times your size," the younger guard said.

"I'll call you when I want him out of here." Piros closed the door. "It's cold outside. I'll warm you up."

"Thank you."

"You think you're funny? Sit down, hog. Here, let me take off your boots. I don't mind doing it for you. I understand humility. I am just a simple village boy." Piros pulled off his boots, then tied his wrists and ankles with leather belts. "Now push your knees between your arms. Don't you want to help Inspector Piros? I want your knees touching your chest." Piros slid a broom handle through the bundle of flesh and pushed him sideways. One end of the broom handle touched the floor. "Do you want to talk?"

"No."

"Say 'sir.' You are not suffering. Don't think that I am a stupid peasant. I know that you think Inspector Piros is stupid, but Inspector Piros is not stupid. I know what's the matter with you. Your arms and legs are too long. See?" Piros pushed a folded blanket between his chest and knees. "Do you want to talk to me now?"

Five minutes passed. He tried to breathe in little swallows, but it didn't help. He flexed different muscles to ease the pain, but that didn't work, either. His circulation was cut off.

"Something tells me that you are suffering now."

He opened his eyes when the bucket of cold water hit his face. Piros was watching him from behind his hands like a child playing peekaboo. He closed his eyes again.

"What are you dreaming about, hog? Do you dream that the Americans will liberate you?"

He kept his eyes closed, feeling a lightness coming over him that made everything easy.

Piros kicked him.

"Are you dreaming of how you will fix me one day?"

The feeling of lightness was gone. He heard his heart banging on his eardrums. He wanted to shout his pain and terror, but there wasn't enough air left in the room.

*   *   *

"Get up, hog," they were shouting at him. He lay unbound on the cobblestone floor, but he couldn't get up. Piros took a step toward him.

"He's had enough, Piros." The guards lifted him by his arms and dragged him outside. The cool night air stopped his nausea, but the pain in his arms and legs remained excruciating.

"Stand up," one of the guards said, letting go of his arm. He hit the ground like a felled tree. They dragged him through the long underground passage to his cell and rolled him inside.

Slowly the pain receded into a dull, constant throbbing. He dragged himself to his metal bed and lay down. He wanted to sleep, but hunger took over with such intensity that sleep was impossible. He was rational enough to know that it was absurd to believe that the hunger pain was pressing his head out of shape so that his eyes would not close. He counted to sixty again and again to keep track of the passing minutes, which were bringing him closer to the morning soup and bread. Then he became confused. Perhaps it was already a hundred times sixty, or a thousand times, or a million times because it led into a thick, black fog.

*   *   *

Political prisoners were never made into trustees. The trustee who carried the bucket with the morning's caraway soup was a criminal sentenced to ten years for armed robbery. He was talking to the guard who distributed the regulation slices of bread.

"Shut your stupid mouth," the guard told the trustee, but it was too late. He had overheard them. It was August already.

"What day is it?" he whispered to the trustee.

"Shut your mouth, Lorant," the guard bellowed. "Do you want me to spill your soup on the floor?"

"No, sir."

The trustee and the guard went to the next cell.

The morning's caraway soup wasn't scorched. The best thing about it was that for half an hour the soup and the slice of bread combined to create an oasis where he didn't need to think about food. He could daydream about escape and crossing the border to Vienna and his arrival at the barbershop on Kärtner Strasse, not far from the Opera House and the Mozart Cafe, where his father had taken him to have his first shave. The trip had something to do with horses and competition, but he could only remember watching his own face being lathered and trying not to laugh. In the mirror he saw his father standing behind the chair, offering a silver flask to the barber.

"Get to work, Lorant." The guard was opening his cell door.

*   *   *

It was more and more difficult to keep the wheelbarrow back when going down hill and to push it up on the run. The difference in the sensation between going down and coming up had disappeared. There was pain in his chest and a constant drumming in his ears. The black dots before his eyes multiplied.

"Don't walk, Lorant. The standing order is to trot."

"Yes, sir." His brain rattled like a forgotten last coin in a piggy bank.

"A big man like you needs a little workout now and then. You need a few calluses on those noble hands."

"Yes, sir." It would do no good to kill the guard. Vipla was no worse than the others. "Comrade Inspector."

"What?"

"Comrade Inspector, I would like your permission to empty my bowels." It was the regulation request for permission to use the latrine.

"Empty your wheelbarrow first. Then you can go."

"Thank you."

"I warn you, I have a watch in my hand," Vipla said.

"Yes, sir. May I have the time, sir?"

"'May I have the time, sir?'" Vipla was imitating his pronunciation. "Shut up, Lorant, and get on with it."

"Yes, sir." He was trotting down the hillside trying to hold back the wheelbarrow. He was almost certain that it wasn't a Saturday. Hangings always took place early in the morning. At the bottom of the hill was a parked car. There was nobody about. He squatted down beside the left front door. The side-view mirror was small and showed only part of his face. The lines across his forehead were deeper, but it was the forehead he knew. Then he noticed the dead, fixed gaze in the small mirror. The eyes were not his eyes. They were looking back at him with the queer emptiness of the insane.

*   *   *

The next morning he still didn't know what day it was — new prisoners who would have known were always quarantined before they were allowed to mix with the general population — but they had not come to hang him, and he had experienced the first miracle of his life: he couldn't bend his right knee.

After roll call he got permission to go to the infirmary. He hobbled as fast as he could to reach the dream world where nobody shouted, and fleas and lice were shut out. The doctor's white coat gave him a sense of security even though the striped trousers of a prisoner showed below it. There were a few other prisoners waiting in line. They had come to get some animal fat for their raw hands. Later they would smear the fat on their slice of bread and eat it, or would trade it for cigarettes.

The doctor, a white-haired young man, looked at his knee.

"You'll have to be hospitalized. Change here. We don't want any lice inside."

He undressed quickly, afraid that somebody or something might stop him from getting into one of the hospital beds. They had sheets on them.

"Ready?"

"Yes." He climbed onto an enamel-covered table. The doctor poured iodine over his knee.

"You know, Lorant," he said, scalpel in hand, "everything in our lives here is painful. I have nothing to give you against that."

It wasn't a bad pain like being kicked, and it didn't even come close to hunger pain. It came fast, like being touched with a sliver of ice. The throbbing pressure in his knee was released. He saw black blood coming from the wound.

"Most of the time I am too late, but you'll be all right." The doctor clamped the incision and bandaged it. "Sit up slowly."

"I'd rather have this every night than be hog-tied."

"Let me help you get into bed. Don't worry about food. You'll get it here. I'll see you tomorrow."

"Thank you." He lay back comfortably on the mattress, adjusting the blanket around his shoulders. Even the blanket had a sheet underneath. It was easy to tolerate the pain in his knee. He began to say the doxology.

When he awoke, he wasn't too tired to think beyond the throbbing pain in his knee. He thought of Budapest: statues, bridges, the hills of Buda, streets, houses, people who walked on streets, went home after work, had wives and children and mothers and fathers. They must have deported his mother from Budapest months ago. All politically incorrect people were deported to the country in the winter to die in unheated barns. On top of being politically incorrect, his mother was also automatically classified as a class enemy. He wondered if she was still alive. When he was twelve, she would allow him to come to the music room when he stayed home from school pretending to be sick, and she would tell the story of the Ring of the Nibelung, the whole cycle, and would sing all the parts, even Alberich's, trying to deepen her mezzo soprano.

When it became too much to think about her, he went to Vienna, down Kärtner Strasse to the barbershop.

*   *   *

He woke up again, feeling the slow throbbing of his knee. Someone was bending over him, pulling on his blanket. It was Tuskos. At the age of fourteen they had been at the same boarding school.

"What are you doing here?"

"Fixing some loose floorboards," Tuskos said.

"I didn't know carpentry was one of your talents."

"It isn't. I'm very keen on survival, though. I need your help."

"What can I do?" He didn't really like Tuskos. "What do you want from me?"

"I want you to get up three days from today and volunteer for kitchen work. If you seem anxious to work, they won't watch you as closely."

"What is this all about?"

"We need your military belt. We are getting out."

At eleven o'clock on the fourth day he was to ask the guard to let him go to the hospital to have his dressing changed, but instead of going to the hospital he was to meet Tuskos in the trees behind the toolshed.

*   *   *

The guard made no objection, and he began to walk toward the hospital, skirted it, and went around to the toolshed. Nobody was in sight. He tried not to think of all the things that could go wrong, not that it really mattered. On the day Comrade Gero arrived, they would hang him. If they caught him now, they would beat him first and then hang him.

He reached the trees and came upon a group of men. One of them was Tuskos. He was changing into a guard's uniform.

"All right, Lorant," he said. "Give me your belt."

He understood now why Tuskos needed him. A guard's uniform wasn't complete without the wide military belt. Tuskos even had a Russian-made burp gun.

"It won't go off. It's made of wood. Uncle Gyula," Tuskos pointed at a middle-aged man, "is the finest carpenter in the world. Let's get going."

They moved in single file, Tuskos in his fake guard's uniform behind them shouting, "Get moving, hogs, get moving," marching toward a small gate cut into the fence to save time when the quarry needed explosives. The storage building for the explosives was outside the fence. Beside the gate a roofed-over watchtower was set up with a guard, machine gun, telephone, and searchlight.

"That's Vipla up there," Tuskos said in a low voice. "He is the only one who wears an air force cap with his guard uniform."

"He is trouble," one of the men said.

"Lorant, you take him out," Tuskos said. "Uncle Gyula, you go with him. It looks better to have two prisoners together. . . . You two fall out," Tuskos yelled. "Get moving, hogs."

The line of men went on marching toward the watchtower, Tuskos cursing behind them.

"What do we do now, Mr. Lorant?" Uncle Gyula whispered. He had bad bruises on his face.

"Stay out of his sight."

There were only a few trees standing, but the weeds were chest high. He walked bent over, trying not to let the weeds signal his movements, remembering lessons from the military academy but even more his father's teaching him to hunt.

"I can't keep up with you." Uncle Gyula was out of breath.

"Lie down here. In ten minutes you can follow me."

"God be with you, Mr. Lorant."

"God be with you, Uncle Gyula." In the watchtower Vipla's back looked like a small black exclamation mark. Then he went on again, trying to avoid the dried-out poppy pods that stood in his way like so many rattles. It was a question of placing one's feet, his father used to tell him.

He smelled cigarette smoke and froze. He was only a few meters away from the staircase — more like a stepladder — set into the middle of the floor of the watchtower. Vipla was leaning over the banister, watching Tuskos herding his charges toward the gate cut into the fence.

"Where are you going?" Vipla shouted.

"I'm taking the hogs for outside work," Tuskos was shouting too. "Come on, hogs, we haven't got all day."

"I have the key up here."

"Throw it down," Tuskos yelled.

"I don't know you," Vipla shouted, "and I don't like you. I'd better check with H.Q. about the assignment."

It was then that he began to move, running up the stairs, his head now above the floor of the watchtower, seeing Vipla half turning, the olive-gray handset of the phone dropping at his feet, fear in his eyes that made him look for a second like them, the prisoners, before recognition dawned and the fear turned into hate.

"Mr. Lorant himself," Vipla said with a triumphant snarl, but he wouldn't let Vipla speak anymore, hating the voice that had drowned him in humiliation for months, that had made him ask to be allowed to use the latrine, that had made him hate himself. His legs were clamped around Vipla's back in a dreadful imitation of Holbein's *Der Totentanz;* his hands, the mirth of the guards, were slowly twisting Vipla's head as if he were trying to twist a large pumpkin off a vine. He heard the sinews give way with a popping sound. He was looking straight ahead and saw in the distance the large, black, ministerial Mercedes-Benz cars like some horrible banded snake heading for the camp. This was the day, the 15th of August, when he must die. He heard the bones crack; then Vipla's bowels let go.

"Get the key to the gate, Lorant," Tuskos was shouting. "Throw it down."

*   *   *

They were behind the storage building, out of sight but still in the act of prisoners-going-out-to-work, like extras in a Passion play, extending the stage into their lives. Then somebody threw down a pick axe and the spell was broken.

"You are on your own now," Tuskos said. "God be with you."

Though not a word was said, the men, communicating insect-like, formed into groups of twos and threes, each unit going in a different direction, not looking at each other as if they were strangers.

"God be with you, Mr. Lorant," Uncle Gyula said, going off with another middle-aged man. There was no danger in waiting for a while. Vipla's body would not be discovered till the next change of the guard. He didn't want to follow the men too closely. They all had hated Vipla, but it was he who had killed him. He wasn't a soldier anymore. He was like Vipla. He was like Comrade Gero.

He began to walk toward the wooded mountains in the direction of Austria. It was almost dark when the claxons began their howl at the camp.

A Bearer of Divine Revelation

Sleeping under one of the Salzach River bridges on the Monschberg side of Salzburg, he had heard the church clocks strike throughout the night. One in particular, just before booming out the time, sounded as if it were a giant's pocket watch being wound up. Every half hour, coinciding with the striking of the church clocks, an American Military Police jeep turned onto the bridge with squealing tires and crossed to the other side that had, he remembered from visits with his mother before the war, only one interesting tourist spot: the Marionettentheater, where three-foot-high puppets performed Mozart operas. It was there that he first saw *The Magic Flute*. On his side of the river was Mozart's house of birth on Getreidegasse, the Festspielhaus, the focus of his mother's visits, the Mozarteum, where every Tuesday music students gave free concerts, and the Mirabell Garden, with its palace-turned-museum, gnome statues, and formal hedges and flower beds, which had been built by an Archbishop of Salzburg for his mistress, Mirabell.

With the sound of out-of-tune cymbals, dustbins were rolled down the steep streets to waiting trucks. As he looked out from under the bridge, it seemed to him that he was peering through the glass side of a gigantic aquarium filled with murky water. The wind rose, swirling around the accumulated trash. There were a few other sleepers under the bridge, invisible under coats, scarves, and shawls that made them seem like mounds of discarded rags. He himself slept in his short Hungarian tank corps leather coat fastened with mismatched civilian buttons, riding britches with leather patches at the knees and seat, and long boots. Shoes and boots were prime targets for thieves. He had sold his only item of value, the sheepskin lining of his coat, when he first made it to Salzburg from the Soviet Zone two months ago.

It was July now, and later in the day it would be pleasantly warm. At first he had lived in a shelter that had been an auxiliary to a hospital during the war. It was nicknamed "Hotel Europa," but he couldn't stand the smell. It was the stench of the back wards of army surgical hospitals where mutilated people waited to die, and he didn't know how to cope with the palpable tension that was as real in the shelter as the sound of generators in a power station. They were all refugees from the Communists, but that did not diminish old nationalist hatreds. There were frequent knifings over real or perceived slights, over simple friendliness toward someone's wife, daughter, or girlfriend of a different ethnic group or nationality, over accusations of theft, or simply because someone was overcome with the miseries of a life that so undervalued them that they were still in limbo in the second year of peace after seven years of war. Hate remained their strongest feeling. He still carried a combat knife hidden in the top of his right boot.

By seven-thirty he was walking down Getreidegasse, a narrow alley formed by an almost continuous wall of two- and three-story houses. Here and there, olive-painted American cars were parked halfway up the sidewalk. The café where he would spend the last of the money he got for the coat lining was between Mozart's house and the Hotel Blue Goose. The café's plastered walls were peach-colored, and the white curtains across its front window were freshly starched. Erica Korp, who was a waitress there, had told him that the famous comedian Hans Ruhman, having passed the denazification board, came every day. He wasn't there today. People dressed in Styer costumes were sitting at small, marble-topped tables on dark bentwood chairs. The parquet under their feet shone like honey, and there was a lovely aroma of coffee and freshly baked rolls and croissants. He sat down at one of the tables in the back.

"Guten Morgen," Erica said. She was wearing a dirndl whose sky-blue top emphasized not only her buxom figure but also the color of her eyes, making her look like a Tyrolean travel-guide illustration.

"Guten Morgen." He had met her in May, when they were both extras in a movie filmed in the Festspielhaus. They were paid off on a Tuesday, their third week on the set, and he had rented the cheapest room in the Blue Goose. It was at the top of the building under the mansard roof. The nearest w.c. was one floor down, and the bathroom was even further away. But all that didn't matter because they were constantly together, even took the bus to Kitzbühel for a day. By Saturday he was dangerously low on money and had to move back to "Hotel Europa" and from there to living under the bridge closest to the cathedral. After that he didn't see much of Erica, who had to go back to work, and he wondered if it was because he had run out of money, or because her father had warned her about Hungarians.

"You could have come to see me," Erica said. "How are you?"

"Fine." He put his hands under the table; they weren't too clean. "I am on my way to Pension Lotte to find out about a job."

"What kind of a job?"

"Deskman. If I get it, I would have a room of my own. You could visit me."

"There is no deskman at Pension Lotte." She put a menu on the table. "And I wouldn't set foot in there even if they did have one."

*   *   *

The street was packed with people on their way to work or to shop, dirndls and Styer costumes mixed with American uniforms that were so well cut that even privates looked like officers. Some of the Americans were lounging on the sidewalks, throwing tennis balls across the street to each other, catching them with big gloves that turned their hands into Mickey Mouse's hands.

The shops on Getreidegasse were filled with loden coats, leather shorts, dirndls, Styer costumes, ski and hiking boots, Tyrolean hats, and linen shirts. He wondered who could afford to buy them at these prices. He wanted a civilian shirt as the first step to being integrated into a new life of peace he knew so little about. He had left the last of his money for Erica, who had told him once that waitresses didn't feel humiliated if their friends tipped them. Not that the price of a good breakfast and a tip would have bought a shirt.

Close to Mirabell Garden was a large hotel, now exclusively used by high-ranking American officers and their families. It was still considered a luxury hotel because hot water was available twice a week. He knew the place well. He had stayed there with his mother in a suite with its own bathroom on their annual musical jaunts. There were four such suites. To accommodate the other rooms there were two bathrooms and two w.c.'s on each floor. The elaborate entrance — mahogany, glass, and polished brass — had a revolving door flanked by two other doors. He didn't want to be seen loitering around the hotel because the MPs would materialize and demand to see his papers, but he had to chance it. Shielding his eyes, he looked through the windowpane, then entered the revolving door. One of the bathrooms on the first floor was just past the staircase. He smelled the steam and the slightly rotting wood and could hear somebody singing. The other bathroom was locked.

On the second floor the first bathroom he came to had just been vacated; the mirror was steamed over, and he appeared as a shadow only vaguely defined. The smell of American toiletries still advertised the former lawful occupant. He locked the door. From his coat pocket he took out a toothbrush, razor, nail brush, and black comb. He placed them on a shelf in front of the mirror, then put the coat over an unpainted wooden chair and pulled off his boots. He found a bar of soap in the bathtub, broke off a piece, and put it in the sink with his underclothes. He shaved, took a bath, and used his dirty shirt for a towel, after which he put it in the sink with his other washing. He dressed in the clean clothes he carried in his coat pocket, gathered up his washing, and went out into the hall, leaving the bathroom door open to let out the steam. Nobody stopped him when he went through the back door of the hotel.

*   *   *

He sat in the sunshine in Mirabell Garden with his washing laid out on the bench beside him. There were only a few people in the park at this time of the day. Salzburg was on an American schedule now. At noon the benches would be filled with people eating lunch. Fat pigeons were already maneuvering on the clipped grass around the benches, rushing first to the right, then to the left, then slowing down like a motorized army group getting ready to ambush the lunch eaters. He ate pigeons when he couldn't get anything else. It wasn't difficult to catch them, but it was very hard to make himself do it. In his first year at gymnasium he and his friend Tibor, the only Calvinists among the forty-two boys in class 1-A, had founded the Four-leaf Clover Club for the sole purpose of feeding pigeons in the park. The club was to be a secret club for four boys, but nobody ever joined them to add two more leaves to the clover. By the second year, when they were twelve years old and could translate Tertullian's *"Non licet esse nos"* into "It's not allowed to us to exist," but not understand its meaning, they had stopped feeding pigeons.

He was folding his washing to put in his coat pocket when the bells rang out as they had every day all over Europe at twelve o'clock since the fifteenth century to celebrate the victory of Hunyadi, the Hungarian general who stopped the Turks from overrunning the West. The park had started to fill up. The pigeons rose into the air in formation, circled once, then landed again. He stood up, draped his coat over his shoulders in hussar fashion, and left the park. He was hungry again.

Milan, a Serb acquaintance, had told him that the Greek Orthodox had set up a soup kitchen and that if they thought he was an Orthodox they would give him a present besides food. Milan had been a fourth-year medical student, then a medical sergeant in General Mikhailovitch's army that fought the Nazis and Tito's Communist army with success. Inexplicably, the British gave their support to Tito, and now Milan slept under a bridge in Salzburg, waiting to emigrate to Australia as a European Voluntary Worker. EVW was headquartered in the old Lehen barracks, and once people were accepted by the host country, they could move into Lehen barracks two weeks before being shipped out and were given rations every two days.

The Greek Orthodox mission was next to the funicular that conveyed passengers to the top of Monschberg to a medieval fort and an outdoor restaurant. The funicular station was a good place to collect American cigarette butts, which always had quite a bit of tobacco left in them that he mixed together and traded for food. Picking up butts made him feel that he had become an instant obscenity.

The mission was housed in what must have been a school. The splintered floors were oiled, the top part of the wall was dirty-white, the lower portion an institutional green which on three sides was edged with coat hooks. The fourth wall bore the pristine outline of the removed blackboard. There was a black iron stove in one corner, a long table with chairs in the middle, a Ping-Pong table at one side. Sitting at a card table by the door was a girl with large black eyes and curly black hair tied with a lilac ribbon. The light coming through the tall windows banished all shadows and framed her into an icon.

"Guten Morgen." He hated to disrupt the silence.

"Guten Morgen." She smiled and put down her book. She had perfect white teeth. "Father Caranasos will be coming with the food soon." She spoke correct but accented German. "And where do you come from?"

"Hungary, by way of the Russian Zone."

"We used to have churches in Budapest," she said.

"And in Szentendre. That's a small town close to Budapest."

"I know. I have seen it on a map." She wrote something in a notebook. "I am related to Father Caranasos. I came to help him during school holidays."

*   *   *

By one o'clock he was the only outsider left in the mission's dining room. He had stayed on because talking with Father Caranasos reassured him that he wasn't just a walking zombie whose life consisted of thinking up elaborate stratagems and lies for survival.

"All right. What is the central question of moral philosophy?" Father Caranasos asked, speaking in cultured German, unlike most of the people he was ministering to, who spoke "D.P. German," the lingua franca of those displaced by war.

"The central question?" He still remembered it. "Why is it better to be just than unjust."

"I see you have read Plato's *Republic,*" Father Caranasos said.

"I had to in school."

Father Caranasos burst out laughing. "Don't sound so mournful." In his early thirties, Father Caranasos was only four or five years older than he was.

"Learning is never a waste of time, my friend," Father Caranasos said. "And speaking of time, I'll have to move on. There is a meeting at two o'clock with the CARE people."

"I shouldn't have taken up your time. Thanks for feeding me." He turned to go.

"Hold on a minute." Father Caranasos opened a cupboard and took out a pumpkin-shaped ball. "This is an American football. It's made of fine leather. I don't know what you can do with it, but I have nothing else to give you. The Greek-Americans out of the goodness of their hearts send packages to help us, but they don't really know what is needed here."

"I can't take it, Father."

"Why not?"

"Because Milan told me . . ."

"I know Milan, yes."

". . . Milan told me that you feed the hungry but gifts are given only to the Orthodox."

"That isn't true."

"And when I came in, I implied to the girl . . ."

"Elena."

". . . that I was Orthodox. I am a Calvinist, Father. I am a Reformed."

"Here, take it." Father Caranasos handed over the football, then reached up and touched his shoulder. "You are even more than that." He patted his shoulder to emphasize the words. "You are a bearer and announcer of the divine revelation."

*   *   *

It took him only half an hour to take the football apart and sell the leather for shoe soles. As he was walking to the trolley stop amidst the noise of the narrow streets, where strange-looking yellow buses packed with American children passed him and where G.I.'s shouted to each other and laughed at jokes he couldn't understand, he heard — perhaps because he wasn't hungry at that moment, and the shrapnel pieces in his body were quiet — he heard in his head, louder than any other sound, Mozart's Piano Concerto in D Minor, heard it so clearly that he could think that it had been bequeathed to him as an inheritance from his old life and feel rich and satisfied.

*   *   *

The trolley stopped almost at the front door of Pension Lotte. The one-story house, a twenties "modern," was built of dark brick. Wrought-iron bars on the windows and the front door gave it a sinister look made worse by a small, oblong sign with the legend OFF LIMITS stuck into the front lawn. He rang the doorbell and waited nervously, knowing that he was being inspected. It wasn't the telltale glint of the sun on binoculars or on the barrel of a gun that told him, but he knew somehow and wanted to throw himself down below the line of windows.

"Yes?" It was a woman's voice.

"I heard you need a janitor."

"Yes." The door opened. "Come in."

He stood staring at her long, Titian-red hair, her green eyes in the pleasantly plump face, her creamy skin, and was unable to move.

She was laughing. "Come in. I am Frau Hemming. Have you never seen a redhead before?"

Frau Hemming led him into a large furnished room that looked like a dining room in an Alpine inn. "Sit down. Have you got any papers?"

"No papers. The Russians took me off the Arlberg Express."

"And you got away without your papers."

"Yes."

"What a mess. . . . Not that it matters to me, unless the Interpol is looking for you. . . . I can give you a small room, and you'll get enough tips to buy your own food. Some of the women who live here might give you something to eat if they like you. Sometimes they like a back rub. Can you give back rubs?"

"Yes, Frau Hemming."

"These women are all refugees. They pay very well for their rooms, but they want privacy. We are off limits, and their friends are Americans. Do you understand?"

"Yes, Frau Hemming."

"When they ask you to do something for them, do it. They tip well. They may ask you to go to the American camp and pick up packages. If you bring back big boxes, you'll get your trolley fare."

"I can't speak English."

"They'll tell you what to say. Your main job will be to put on the padlocks."

"Yes, Frau Hemming." He was mystified.

"Another thing. Your name will be George. The Americans are used to calling the janitor George."

*   *   *

His life as George the janitor lasted exactly six weeks, after which he was fired for not letting out Marika Kocsis's American sergeant, who should have been at his duty station at 0.500 hours but who showed up at 1300 hours. The sergeant was restricted to barracks, which meant Marika had to use her savings to survive. Marika had become his friend. She was his own age, had graduated from a very good girl's school in Budapest, and liked classical music. They had gone twice to the Mozarteum's Tuesday afternoon free student concerts, and he held her hand and even thought he was in love with her but decided that he couldn't be.

It was all very complicated at the pension. Because Pension Lotte was off limits, the MPs had to be paid off, but even so it was his duty to put padlocks on the doors when the Americans were visiting so that the MPs wouldn't check those rooms. The Americans would tell him when they had to leave so that he would know when to take off the padlocks. The Americans usually gave him a pack of cigarettes which he sold on the black market. Pall Malls brought in the most money. A further complication was that Frau Hemming always wanted him to give her back rubs. Most of the guests knew this and made faces at him behind Frau Hemming's back. Marika knew it too. Then on that fateful morning three days ago his alarm clock didn't go off — most nights he didn't get more than three or four hours' sleep — and he was fired.

At first he was quite relieved to be back under the bridge, where life was simpler. He even went to the Lehen barracks to sign up as a European Voluntary Worker. It would be hard to survive here in the winter, and it was already the second week in September. With any luck, in a few weeks he would be on his way to a British coal mine or cotton mill. In the meantime, he had to find food. Four days after he left Pension Lotte, he started getting dizzy spells. Eating every day for six weeks had stretched his stomach, and he was very hungry. His brain had slowed down to the point where he couldn't think of any schemes that would result in food or remember the staggered schedules of the soup kitchens. With his rolled-up coat under his head, he went back to sleep.

*   *   *

The triumphant pealing of the midday bells woke him. He was lying on his side under the bridge, watching the sun turning the Salzach River into a silver-scaled snake of mythical proportions. He got up, folded the newspaper he used as a ground sheet and hid it under chunks of cement, then brushed his teeth. He vaguely remembered hearing about the charitable nuns when he first arrived in Salzburg. Their cloister was on the Marionettentheater side of the river.

An MP was directing traffic with the concentration and skill of an orchestra conductor. Most of the pedestrians were civilians who seemed to be hurrying across the bridge on an urgent rescue mission. The Americans ambled — even in mufti they were recognizable as Americans — as if victory allowed them to pause, stretch, look around, and play the tourist. He too was playing the tourist and turned back to study the green cupolas of the cathedral and look up at the fort crowning Monschberg. The funicular cars were slowly ascending and descending like some newfangled angels, and he wondered what God would promise now to the millions of new wanderers.

He walked by the post office and, seeing the Austrian flag, remembered the swastikas flying when Salzburg had ceased to be Mozart's town and had become Hitler's.

The cloister was a disappointment. It looked like its neighbors, a nineteenth-century, grimy apartment building. He had expected something medieval where a beggar would look natural. His mother was always keen on style and appropriateness. One wing of the brown front door was propped open by several tall trash cans. He went in, up the worn stairs, smelling the freshly washed stone floor, the dampness communicating poverty that no amount of scrubbing could erase, and came into a dim vestibule. At first he felt, more than saw, the large crucifix with the writhing, full-size representation of Christ, the meager light coming from an unseen window touching the crown of thorns, throwing the face into shadow. Beyond the cross he descended the six stairs that led down to a single, huge oak door without a knob or lever of any kind. Incongruously, there was an oblong button attached to the door frame like a fat white grub. He pushed it and heard a bell ring, a muted, ordinary bell such as the bells they had in his parents' house to summon the servants, bells that he would not be allowed to ring until he was twenty-one because the servants were grown people who earned their keep, and he was only a boy who had to learn humility. By the time he was twenty-one, he was far away, sitting in a tank, half mad with fear and concentration, trying to survive. When he went home on leave, their house had been bombed to smithereens.

He waited, standing in front of the door, thinking that his humility training finally bore fruit in restraining him from ringing again, and he began to laugh. A small window opened in the upper part of the door.

"What do you want?"

"I am hungry, sister." He saw the habit, not the face.

"So is everybody," she said and closed the window.

He sat down on the top step, too tired to move. The shadow of the cross, elongated and hunchbacked, lay on the floor. He turned his head to look at the pain-racked body on the cross, thinking that this was reality.

"Bring back the vessel when you are through." The nun was at the opening again, holding out a restaurant-size tin can that once held vegetables, a spoon, and a thick slice of brown bread.

"I will. Thank you, sister." He stumbled, almost falling.

"Watch out," the nun said.

He held the can to his chest, feeling its marvelous heat, the smell of the soup taking over every thought. He was sitting again on the top of the stairs, drinking from the can, feeling the hot liquid filling up the empty spaces, clearing the fog from his head. He put the can down beside him, picked up the bread from his lap with both hands, and broke it. Christ had died for him, died in real agony a real death. He was cramming the bread into his mouth, crying and chewing at the same time, overcome by a terrible sadness, pity for God, who chose him and relied on him to be a bearer and announcer of the divine revelation.

A D-minor Fugue

FUGUE. *n.* 1: polyphonic musical composition in which
one or two themes are repeated or imitated by succes-
sively entering voices and contrapuntally developed in
a continuous interweaving of the voice parts 2: a dis-
turbed state of consciousness in which the one affected
performs acts of which he appears to be conscious but
of which on recovery he has no recollection

The fog smelled of soot and the discharge from the cotton mills. It
took its coloration from the black October night and the yellow so-
dium lights that bathed the freight yard with the sunrise of plastic reality.

The room the foreigner slept in had only three walls. In fact it was
really just a large landing, a turning of the staircase leading up to the at-
tic in a house among a row of houses in a Lancashire mill town.

Out in the fog an engine shunting freight cars transformed itself
into a nightmare. The whistle alerted the border guards; then the
sound of screaming ended in a crash that built the fourth wall and
filled the room with suffocation. Then nothing, and the sound that had
become nothing speeded up, faded, to come back again louder and
faster, a D-minor fugue.

He pulled a string reaching down from the ceiling beside his cot. The naked bulb gave out a faint, sick light, turning his trousers hanging from a nail into a horrible, grotesque shadow. He was sweating, though his breath was white.

For all of them during the last minutes there was always the fear of pain, but for him there was the other fear too: he had seen them stain their trousers, and he had not wanted to look obscene at the hour of his death. He had already lost his soul earlier by signing and saying whatever he was told to sign and say because there was still hope for the body. It had been for nothing. He was alive only because his name was way down in the alphabet.

He pulled the string. The landing felt warmer in the dark. Then the whistle screamed.

No, he thought, no, but he didn't turn on the light. He was afraid to look again at the shadow on the wall. It reminded him of the waiting for his own turn and of them, grotesque and obscene, swinging and twisting like pendulums in broken clocks. With some of them just a few years before he had been memorizing portions of Titus Livius's *Punic Wars*, shouting "Hannibal ante portas!" laughing and laughing because the killings of antiquity seemed funny to sixteen-year-olds.

*   *   *

"Rise and shine!" Mr. Turner shouted, standing on the bottom step of the staircase.

"Thank you," he said, getting up from the cot. Every morning for the past six months, ever since the Ministry of Labour had sent him to Lancashire to be a weaver in a cotton mill, Mr. Turner had been his first link with humanity. Wages were better in the mines, but the union objected to foreigners, saying that their thick accents endangered mine safety.

"The porridge smells lovely," Mr. Turner announced, wrinkling his nose like an oversized rabbit. "You'd better hurry up, John, before I eat it all."

"Aye," he said, hoping to sound like Mr. Turner. Of course his name wasn't John, but that didn't matter anymore. At first he had resented being named like a new dog, but later he understood that it wasn't done from malice.

He looked into a shard of a mirror Mrs. Turner had given him and decided not to shave even though the stubble under his chin was itchy. Mr. Turner shaved only on Saturdays and Wednesdays. He wanted to be like them, the people who belonged, who felt easy with each other in the pubs, shops, at work. The people who were free. Not like him, who was to be under the Ministry of Labour for seven years, till he became naturalized. That was five years away. And what then?

He pulled on his socks, then his clogs. The tops were made of black leather.

A penniless foreigner stayed down, and all he could look forward to would be the free specs, dentures, and hearing aid, and if he could get in, a finish at an almshouse. Alone, of that he was certain. What girl would marry him? As long as he was young they would go with him into parks, under railroad bridges, even into doorways, but marry him . . . never. He was a bloody foreigner. Nothing could or would change that.

As he was going downstairs to have his breakfast, he was thinking that he couldn't marry one of them, either. "My dear," he remembered his mother saying, "it is always the woman who sets the tone in the house. For the sake of your future children it is most important to marry the proper girl."

"I suppose she must like baroque music and be able to sing all the solo parts in *Der Tag des Gerichts*?" he had said.

"The choruses as well," she said, and they had laughed.

"Come on, lad," Mr. Turner said. "Get at it."

"Good morning," he said.

"Mornin'." Mrs. Turner was bending over the fireplace, reaching for the blackened kettle. "Nasty morning."

As if to underscore her statement, a pompous voice issuing from the wireless intoned, "Visibility poor."

*   *   *

It was dark outside. The air was raw with a new acridness that made the town into a gigantic bedroom, its door and windows tightly shut, trapping inside the night smells.

"John," Mr. Turner said.

"Aye?" He tried not to gag. The cinder underfoot plotted their progress across the tiny yard. To the left stood a slightly squashed dustbin, a small ghost bowing farewell.

"The Missus mustn't find out about the doggies."

"No, she mustn't," he agreed. He couldn't quite see Mr. Turner's nose, but he was sure that it moved up and down, a rabbit coming face to face with a head of lettuce.

"Right, lad. This time the doggies run right. I owed you five pounds, and here's two bob extra for your trouble."

"That was no trouble." He handed back the two shillings.

"You don't want it?"

"No, thanks."

"Righto, John," Mr. Turner said. "Ta. Ta very much."

They were in the alley, turning into the street toward the sound that wasn't loud or harsh but went on and on like a toothache that can be stopped only by a bigger pain. He hung back a moment, seeing the darker shapes of people in the gray light shuffling their clogs slowly, steadily toward the mills like a defeated army on an endless retreat.

"Come on, lad," Mr. Turner said.

Some of the men in the ranks greeted them by jerking their heads, but nobody said a word. There was no need for speech. In their misery they had become as one. And he belonged with them.

*   *   *

The trick was to keep the rhythm going. Shove in the bobbin, start the loom, step left to the next loom, and repeat and repeat and repeat. The proper rhythm slowed the pendulums' swinging and twisting.

He was moving about his four looms, singing. Nobody could hear him in the noise the looms made; besides, the people plugged their ears to keep from going deaf.

He changed his song to *repetere et repetere et repetere* because it gave a more accurate rhythm and because he knew that if he went on singing *repeat and repeat and repeat* he would end up pulling out his pocket-knife to cut across the yarn to free the poor machine of its burden. The yarn turned into calico, and as he watched for faults, the calico turned into a wide, flat river, iced over and covered with snow to hide the mutilated dead who had been thrown into it in between the parliament building on the Pest side and the wharf on Buda.

The wharf had been paved with cobblestones that fitted the summer evenings and the river smell perfectly, so that to his astonishment girls actually wanted to kiss him, though he was thin and tall and had one eyebrow higher than the other. Now in his mind the girls were only damp hands wilting the flowers he had brought. The wilting flowers used to make him feel guilty, but that was before all the bridges were blown up and the river iced over and covered with snow to hide the bodies caught like driftwood on the wreckage.

Somebody touched his shoulder. Though the touch was gentle, it took all his willpower to keep his hands down and turn slowly.

"Three ha'pence," the girl standing beside the tea wagon mouthed. The only way to communicate was to lip-read. He put down the coins next to the shiny urn and reached for one of the thick mugs.

"Ta," he mouthed, turning back to his machines. The fear of hurting one of them had made him sweat. The pendulums speeded up.

He changed bobbins. The tea was sloshing to the rhythm of the looms.

"The brew tha-a-t cheers," he sang at the top of his lungs, "but never, no never in-ebri-ate-s-s-s." The tea in his mug was already covered with lint. He took a swig. The lint tasted the same as the tea.

*   *   *

Perhaps he already had an inkling of it when he pulled the cotton wool from his ears, feeling dizzy, as if he needed the combined clattering of looms to keep him upright; his head was now a seashell that retained the roaring of the looms. Certainly by the time he had shaved and washed he knew that he would not go back to the mill for the afternoon. He had the money. He wasn't going to wait. If he waited any longer, Mr. Turner's dogs would come in dead last again, and he would borrow the money back. It had already happened twice before. This afternoon he was going to buy a mackintosh in Burnley at the Fifty Shilling Tailors. Greenish olive. All the men in the mills wore greenish-olive macs.

Outside on a low wall a striped cat stood, X-ing its legs. As he neared, it began to purr, sounding like a perfectly tuned motorbike. One day he would have a 500 cc. bike or a three-wheeler Morgan with a windscreen like in the old, open cockpit planes. He would wear goggles and romantic leather headgear that would cover his black, un-English hair. Or he could drive a red MGTC. The younger of the two dentists had one, and everybody thought him sporting.

The red double-decker stopped. He got on and went upstairs to the front seat. Sitting alone up against the windscreen was the next best thing to driving a red MGTC. He wondered how old he had to be to feel and think like the grown-ups.

The bus turned left by the town hall, where the dances were held on Saturdays. He wasn't a beer drinker or a dart player, so Mr. Turner, who indulged in both, had told him about the dances. The first time he had gone to the Saturday-night hop, he had thought that Mr. Turner had sent him, out of misguided helpfulness, to a bawdy house. The town hall's banquet room used for the dances was a long rectangle, with chairs arranged around the walls, on which sat young men with girls perched on their laps. The girls' faces under the thick makeup were masklike, and they looked bored. One of them smiled at him, and when the music began she left her young man's lap and went up to him.

"I didn't recognize you," he said, relieved. He had come to the right place. This was where the Saturday-night dances were held.

"A bit o' makeup does wonders for a girl," the tea-wagon girl said. She was smoking a cigarette and eating chocolate at the same time. "Care to dance?"

He loved to float and swirl with the American music that made him free of the cotton mills and the reality of the town, but no man could float and swirl by himself. The last men to do that and not be frowned upon were King David and perhaps his own father moving to the sound of a gypsy band, but even he had to pretend to be drunker than he actually was.

The tea-wagon girl's name was Mavis. She liked to dance very close, and he had to be careful not to show how much he enjoyed being close to her even though he couldn't stand her when she was talking.

Her boyfriend tapped him on the shoulder, but Mavis sent him away, which he didn't seem to mind, sitting down on one of the empty chairs, waiting patiently for her return. Without question the English were the most civilized people on earth.

After the dance Mavis went off with her boyfriend and was sitting in the car when the boyfriend tried to run him down. The next Saturday he left the dance with an older girl, a nurse. They had to climb over the closed park gate to get to the glass shelter. When he climbed back out, a car and a motorcycle with a sidecar were waiting for him. The third Saturday and all the subsequent Saturdays had nothing to do with floating and swirling to the American music that had made him feel free of the cotton mills and the reality of the town and the reality of his own life. He understood Mavis now and the uses of shadows under the railroad bridge. He understood that he was being used and that he was using them too, even the boyfriends' hate that allowed him to cleverly bend thick wires into the required shapes the way he had been trained to do and put them under the boyfriends' cars and motorcycles and then watch the tires burst when they pulled smartly away. Sometimes this stopped the pendulums for days, though he knew that he would have to kill to stop them completely. He was back to normal, living in hate and danger, theirs and his own.

When he got off the bus at Burnley — he was the last to get off; the sign on the back had already been changed — he also understood that he was starved for love. He was starving to death.

*   *   *

He came back from Burnley wearing his stiff, immaculate, greenish-olive mac that was too new to be taken to work; besides, he was pretending to be a tourist from the Continent. Nobody had ever been deported for taking the afternoon off.

He walked by the soot-begrimed stone houses that looked like an overdone movie set for *Les Misérables,* then the square, all gray with the town hall and the Golden Lion facing each other, weights in a giant wheel. A double-decker with its engine shut off waited for the turnaround time to end. The driver was on his way toward the town's only public convenience. A dark barrel of a woman, the conductress, was leaning against the side of the bus.

"Hello, Ducky," he said.

"Hullo. Want a cig?"

"No, thanks." Then, remembering his new mac that was supposed to give him the proper coloration, he dropped the continental tourist and took the offered cigarette.

"Ta, ta very much."

Ducky was the older sister of the nurse he had met at his second Saturday dance when he still had his illusions. She was pathetic with her thick pancake makeup, unbecoming dresses, and worse cinema mannerisms. He felt guilty because he couldn't see her as a sex object, when all she wanted to do was to wait for dark to walk down to the railroad bridge.

Though he was a weaver like most of them, the adults saw in him a difference that seemingly could not be overcome and would separate him for the rest of his life, as if he were a lion in a zoo behind a chasm built to protect the public.

He had reached the park. The gate was open, and there were older people sitting in the glass shelter. The grass here was still Watteau-green. As he walked by the shelter, he jerked his head around in greeting, but it didn't work right. He looked more like a poison victim in his death throes than a north countryman greeting his brethren. One had to be born in Lancashire to be able to do it properly.

He was standing close to a large oak when he saw her. She was sitting on a park bench with a book in her hands. She differed from the girls he had seen at the Saturday-night dances. She didn't use any makeup, and there was something else that he was unable to define now that she was looking at him and his heartbeats had become so noisy that he couldn't think straight. He didn't even have time to sort himself out, and the weaver in the greenish-olive mac, the strange-familiar self whose existence he would not allow, and the continental tourist were all jumbled together in his heartbeats.

"Hullo," she said. She smiled, and he knew somehow that this was the way she had smiled at the old people when she had come into the park by the glass shelter.

"Are you a ballerina?" There was a picture of a ballerina on the cover of her book.

"Oh, no." Sudden sorrow turned her eyes dark. "I started too late. I'm too old ever to be a first-class dancer."

"Too old?" He was astonished. She looked sixteen. Maybe seventeen.

"You have to start when you're seven or eight," she said. "I only started a few years ago. It's terribly difficult, you know. . . . Are you German?"

106

"No, I am not." He was surprised by his own vehemence. He believed he had done with nationalistic pride, that he was beyond all that and would not be offended if a stranger assigned him to another group.

"My mother would have minded, but I don't really care where people come from. I like strangers. I have an uncle who lives in Devon."

"Did you think me a foreigner even before I opened my mouth?"

"Yes," she said. "Who do you think you look like?"

"I look like all the other blokes at the mill. I just bought this mac in Burnley," he said. Her laughter swooped up and around trees, a swallow's dance at sundown.

"You look foreign-intrigue even in your Burnley mac." The swallows were swooping around him, touching his face with soft wingtips, and for no reason at all he wanted to cry. It had happened to him once as a boy, lost in the woods for three hours. Then suddenly he had recognized some of the trees, and he was crying with relief. He was home.

*   *   *

"You didn't tell me your name yesterday," he said. They were sitting on a park bench as far away from the tennis courts and the bowling green as it was possible to be. There was lint on his trousers. He had come straight from the mill.

"One's given name is a serious matter. You don't just hand it out like playbills," she said. She was wearing a knitted cap with brown designs that made her look like a friendly elf. "Remember the burning bush where He gave His name?"

"Do you believe it?"

"Yes," she said matter-of-factly. It was then that he realized how young she was. He would have probed first to find out the other's belief or the lack of it before committing himself. He too believed but was afraid because God, whom he knew from observing from behind another kind of bush, might kill him or anybody he loved. There was a line drawn, and on the other side even the cattle were to be killed. Joshua had been given his orders.

"Which is your church?"

"St. Margaret's."

"Catholic?"

"Church of England," she said, as if this should be self-evident, as if there were no denominations, not to speak of religions, other than the C of E. "And my name is Jessica. Jessica Gordon . . . I hate it."

"Jessica," he said. "Jessica."

*   *   *

"We look all right together," he said. They were passing a shopwindow. Jessica came up to his shoulder. "I am not too tall for you."

"We'll never get to the pictures if you keep stopping all the time." She was smiling up at him. "Come on." She linked his arm and pulled him away from the shopwindow. From across the street two girls in school uniforms were waving at them. When Jessica noticed, they began to shout, "Jessica, Jessica! Hullo, Jessica."

"Do you know them?"

"Yes," she said, turning her head. "They go to Counthill Grammar. Silly schoolgirls."

To him the girls looked the same age as Jessica. He wondered again how old she actually was and if she really was a typist in the mill office. He had never seen her there, but then he didn't go to the office often.

They turned the corner.

"Oh, look at the queue," she cried. "We'll never get in."

"I don't mind."

"I thought you wanted to see that new American singer."

"I wanted to see you."

"Oh, you silly thing." She reached for his hand and held it tight.

"People can see us," he said.

"What difference does it make?"

The queue behind them had grown to the corner. Jessica was still holding his hand. He was happy beyond words; besides, he didn't like to talk in public. He didn't want people to hear his accented English. They would all stare at him. Jessica shouldn't be humiliated on his account. Nobody in the queue knew him; he was sure of that.

"Hey, Jessica, thanks for saving our places." Three boys, none of them looking older than sixteen, surrounded Jessica. "Let us in, eh?" one of them whispered.

"No," she said. "Go to the end like anyone else. Anyway, I am not by myself."

It was then that they first noticed him.

"You mean him? You are going to the pictures with him?"

"I am not talking to you anymore, Brian Ogden," Jessica said.

"Oh, aren't you?" The boy (he had reddish-blond hair and was taller than the other two) turned to his friends. "I know who he is. He's one of them foreigners they took on at the mill. Aren't you, mister? I've heard all about you from Mavis Sommers's boyfriend. . . . You want to hear what he's done, Jess? I can tell you all about him."

He didn't remember pulling out his knife. He was standing a little aside from them all, knife in his right hand, his left gently gesturing. There was exultation in him. He would stop the boy with the reddish-blond hair from speaking ever again and that would stop the pendulums and the pain that came from fear that this would happen sometime because it was happening now.

"Stop it!" Jessica was screaming. "Stop it!"

*   *   *

He crossed the square. Both the town hall and the Golden Lion were closed. It was Sunday. Now even the houses gave an impression of being closed against outsiders. He wondered if there was a special Sunday look and feel to an English town or if it was just that he was usually shut up in the mill at this time of the day.

He should have gone to Leeds. In a large town he could easily blend in. Whenever he went to Manchester, Leeds, or Burnley, he thought of the trip as coming up for air. But he hadn't gone today. Since they had first met, he had had to see her daily to stave off the terrible hopelessness that gripped him when he wasn't with her, though even when walking at her side or sitting in the park next to her he was conscious of time and the inevitability of separation. And today he was even more afraid than ever — afraid she might never speak to him again. Last night in his dark room, listening to Mrs. Turner's clock downstairs, he had felt certain that beyond the ticking clock there was nothing.

He was passing the tobacco-and-sweets shop with the hand-printed sign SORRY, NO CIGARETTES, NO MATCHES, PASHA ONLY in the window when he saw Jessica coming toward him. He was flooded with so much joy that it frightened him.

"Jessica!"

Jessica's father, who was the fishmonger on Alma Road, recognized him and rolled his head in greeting. Her brother and sister were staring at him. Her mother looked through him.

"Jessica," he called again. She walked by looking straight ahead, humming a little tune he didn't recognize, then the sound of the world was turned down or had been lost somewhere because he couldn't hear anything. He was standing utterly alone, caught fast on something resembling the mechanical stairs he had first seen in a Burnley department store that moved him, trapped in this world of time, toward an overwhelming, suffocating, final meaninglessness. There was no help for him. The line was drawn, and he was facing the dark, merciless shape standing behind Joshua.

The street was lit up by an October sun, as if a hidden searchlight had been switched on to dispel the usual murk and show everything clearly. He was pinned down, the unfortunate victim of a thoughtless child whose hobby, this week, was the collecting of Heteroptera. He wanted to scream but knew it wouldn't do any good, remembering the screamers and the mute ones moving equally and inexorably toward their identical fate with no more meaning than could be read on the face of a broken clock that still showed the hour it had stopped.

The town-hall clock began to whir, but it was drowned out by the church bells announcing matins. He wrenched himself around. Jessica was walking ahead of him, her hands turned out at an elegant angle as if readying for a run that would end in a graceful, soaring leap. It was then that he noticed something strange about her. She was wearing a uniform. A schoolgirl's uniform.

*   *   *

Sweating with anxiety, he carefully moved through the emotional minefield of smells and sights. Like a signal lamp opening its shutter, the sun came in through the stained-glass windows, the red and gold touching the carpet, showing up the pale blue for what it was — dust gray. The kneelers, worn at the edges, were littered with spineless Books of Common Prayer and hymnals. The carved reredos behind the altar, the massive oak pulpit, the brass eagle adorning the lectern all showed Victorian gentility turned shabby.

The heavenly semaphore blinked again. Dusk hid the marble memorials around the walls.

"John," a voice whispered. A chunky woman was moving sideways in the pew to make room for him.

"Ducky?"

"Yes, it's Ducky." She grinned at him. "We are all here."

"Here beginneth . . ." the priest intoned.

He could see neither Ducky's nurse-sister nor her parents, and wondered what Ducky had meant. Then he saw Jessica looking at him shyly from across the aisle and became even more confused.

"And when he was come near," the priest read, "he beheld the city, and wept over it. . . ."

He noticed Mr. Turner wrinkling his nose at him; then the words
— these strange, foreign words — touched him, and he was aware
that for the first time in his life he could hear without distortion and
that He who had wept over Jerusalem, and who was somehow standing beside him now, wept for this town also, for all of them living here
tied to the mills, surrounded by acrid air, the noise of looms, and the
dye-distorted, hideous streams that resembled blood vessels on a
crudely colored anatomical chart. He dared not look up, not because
he feared to encounter again the dark, menacing shape he thought he
had glimpsed or the absolute emptiness that he had seen or had been
dragged through by a continually accelerating escalator, but because
he felt unworthy to behold Him.

*   *   *

They entered the park walking close to each other, but without holding
hands. He was afraid to speak, wondering how he could tell her or anyone that just a few minutes ago he had seen a time of endless dimen-
sion where he was loved and was forgiven and where he himself could
forgive.

"This is where I first saw you, Jessica," he said.

"No, it was that other bench."

"Are you sure?"

"Yes."

They passed the green-painted bench, then turned onto the path
that led to the glass shelter.

"I am sorry about the pictures . . . about last night," he said. "I'm
glad I didn't hurt anybody."

"It doesn't matter." She had been walking with her head down,
but now she looked up at him. "Do you like my uniform? I don't mind
it really, except the white socks. They make your legs look fat."

"You look beautiful and your legs are not fat." He was relieved to
hear her prattle again and reached out for her hand.

"I'm sorry I told all those lies about being a typist and every-thing," she said. "You must think I'm silly."

"I think you are very young," he said, knowing that he shouldn't have said it.

"Well, I'm not. I'm sixteen. I'll be seventeen soon."

"When is your birthday?" he asked, thinking that at sixteen he was still at the gymnasium in Budapest, unaware of the horrors that were waiting just a few years away. His biggest nightmare then had been memorizing Titus Livius's *Punic Wars.* He had to in order to "sharpen the brain." He wondered how many of his classmates with sharpened brains were still alive. He still remembered snatches of "the greatest war ever fought" that always brought back the distorted faces and bodies that turned into twisting pendulums.

"What are you thinking about? You look sad," she said.

"It seems so long ago, when I was sixteen. We still had our villa in the country then. My mother used to sing in the evenings." Suddenly he remembered something. "Can you sing?"

"Of course. I am in the school choir."

"Do you know *Der Tag des Gerichts?*"

"It sounds German — what is it?"

"Telemann. You must learn it. It's very important." And he began to hear the chorus, his mother among them, echoing the eschatologi-cal promise *The Lord is coming,* the music building toward the fourth and final contemplation and John's voice: "The Lamb that was slain is worthy to receive adoration." "Holy is our God, the Lord Sabaoth," he sang with the choir.

"I can easily learn it," Jessica said.

"I know. I knew it when I first met you," he said, not noticing that the pendulums that had swung and twisted in his head for so long had disappeared as if they had never been.

At a Certain Angle

The Manchester fast train pulled in with a rush, the station's glass
roof containing the sound and at the same time distorting the
voice coming through the loudspeaker so that the broad Devon dia-
lect had become the cry of a muezzin calling the faithful. The man
standing at the edge of the platform, a long way from the train because he had been facing the wrong direction, was swaying a little.
The staccato explosions of slammed-open carriage doors made him
turn around.

The carriages were spilling people onto the platform. He walked
toward the train, his path clogged with people in small groups flowing
toward the exit presided over by the ticket collector, the last hurdle to
be surmounted by those who, unlike himself, had been found. To meet
here in Exeter, three hundred miles from their homes, to find each
other, needed a miracle. It was then that she called his name.

She was standing in front of him with her face uplifted, waiting
exactly as he had imagined she would, as he had seen it over and over
again in his head — a short film of instructions with the "on" button
stuck.

"You taste like whiskey," she said.

"And you taste like iron. You haven't eaten, have you?" They were
walking toward the exit.

"I couldn't."

"I couldn't, either."

"But you could drink, couldn't you?"

"Yes." He was feeling in his change pocket for the platform ticket. With his other hand he was holding on to her.

"Why?"

"I like the taste, and people are more friendly in a pub."

"Those aren't the only reasons, are they?"

"I didn't think you would come," he said.

"How could I not come?"

"Just a moment, miss," the ticket collector said. "This ticket is punched *for* Manchester, not *from* Manchester." He held the ticket out for them to see.

"My wife just got off the Manchester train. If you want to punch something, punch this one." He shoved his three-penny platform ticket under the man's nose. "My wife is tired."

"Please, Andre," she said. "He is only trying to do his job."

"All right then, miss," the ticket collector said, "go on. Go on, miss."

"She is no miss. She is my wife." He wanted to hit out. Just to hit the man once.

They were through the barrier. In the station buffet an urn huffed white steam. His car was parked in front of the buffet.

"Why do you have to lie to strangers who couldn't care less what we are to each other?"

"I think of you as my wife."

"You frighten me. I never know what you might do next. There is something to be said for civilized English behavior."

"Then why did you come?"

"I wanted to O.D.," she said.

"You wanted what?" They were standing outside, on the street. The mismatched architecture was a memorial to the people who had died in an urban renewal of German bombs.

"I wanted an overdose of you," she said.

*   *   *

In Canterbury the houses were small and hunchbacked in their weather-beaten, soft colors, giving the empty street its medieval character. He felt safe to be here with her in the twelfth century, even though this made the murder of Thomas à Becket just a half a mile from where they stood a fresh enormity.

"We ought to go in," she said. He didn't answer, trying to stay in the twelfth century where she was his wedded wife, because in the reality of the twentieth she was married to a branch manager of the National Westminster Bank, Ltd. "We ought to go in," she said again.

"Yes." He was conscious of their red-brick, Georgian hotel waiting for them. "Why are you crying?"

"I keep thinking how sad it is that we're spending our lives this way. Out of a whole week I see you for fifteen hours at the most." She was crying hard now against his chest. Over her head he saw the traffic flowing in a circle like flotsam in a flooded river.

"We'll be together for two days," he said. "This isn't Lancashire. In Canterbury I am not just a foreign art teacher. Here I can be anything you want me to be. I could kneel in front of you and yell 'Vitam et sanguinem' at the top of my voice to make you my queen, and it would be proper, or I could fling down my mac, for you to walk on, though I would rather offer you my life and my blood." This made her cry harder. He was completely bewildered. "What is it?"

"It's you. No wonder people are always staring at you. You are an overstatement."

"Please," he said. "Please. When I have more English clothes I'll be all right."

"'When I have more English clothes,'" she mimicked him. They began to laugh, holding each other.

"I don't want anything else," he said. "I don't want anything else."

*   *   *

"Did you pray for deliverance?" she asked. They were caught up in the midst of a West German tour whose members had materialized from the far corners of the cathedral as soon as the service had ended.

"Deliverance from what?"

"Me," she said.

"How could I?" He had expected choirs of heavenly voices praising God, and the call for the heavy laden and all that travail, and not two tired clergymen reading the Evening Prayer.

"Didn't I just hear you say with the others, 'And grant, et cetera, et cetera, that we may hereafter live a godly, righteous, and sober life'? Or shall I quote you the communion service? 'We do earnestly repent and are heartily sorry for these our misdoings.'"

"You are not a misdoing to me," he said. "You are what makes me want to go on living, even in exile." He was looking at her profile, her small, perfect ears, her soft, shiny hair, and felt love vibrating inside him like a hummingbird.

"I wish we hadn't gone to the service," she said. "I feel such a hypocrite."

"Then what must you think of me?" It was chilly outside, but not with the cryptlike chill of the cathedral. The narrow buildings housing shops and eating places on both sides of Christchurch Gate crowded each other, fighting for space.

"Somehow it's all right for you, it's different, but when you drag me in to the service as though God's your personal friend and we're all going to have tea together, it gets to be a little too much. I keep thinking of the Commandments . . . or don't you think they apply to us?"

"Of course they apply. But they were given as a help, not as a whip." He was filled with despair. Cut off from God, he could not be a part of the community and would have to remain a stranger for the rest of his life, set apart by an accent that in the end would creep even into his mother tongue to mark him any place on earth.

"God doesn't allow you to pick and choose," she said.

"I thought you didn't believe." There were German tourists around them, and he was surprised that he could understand them so well. He hadn't spoken German since the Ministry of Labour had permitted him to leave the coal mine so that he could be employed as an art teacher at Fleetwood Grammar. "You said there was no God, only frightened people."

"I can't see you going to church and not trying to give me up. I feel awful when you make me go," she said.

"We go everywhere together."

"It wasn't necessary to stay for Evensong."

"I wanted you to hear the liturgy. To share it. You always give me books to read."

"I know all the services by heart. And most of the hymns too, thank you."

"Then what is wrong?"

"You," she said. He was holding her tight, thinking of dying to stop the pain, thinking that suicide was less of a sin than keeping her away from God.

"I will go away. You will never have to see me again. I will go to America."

"You don't understand." She sounded frightened. "I lie sometimes. . . . I haven't been to church since I got married. You are not my stumbling block. . . . You see, I know all about it." She was on tiptoe, stretching to kiss his face. "I feel closer now than I have been since I was a child. And more guilty. I think now I know what love is." They were passing a Roman Catholic church that, in contrast with the cathedral and the houses squatting around it, seemed quite modern.

"Then you know Him," he said.

"No, you're wrong. God is like Grandma was: she took me to the pictures only when I was good and did what she wanted me to do. . . . Would you like to go in? Grandma was a Roman Catholic."

*　　*　　*

The dark office building opposite their window reminded him of an empty honeycomb. He had left the curtains open to let in the street light. Tomorrow morning he must take her to Exeter station and then drive back to Fleetwood. They would meet on Monday at school as colleagues, and he would cease to be himself. The others would transform him into the charming but rather strange art master who could not be trusted with anything as serious as the making of a pot of tea.

He was looking at her profile, which wrenched his heart whenever he saw it at a certain angle where her hair, tight against her skull, left her ears uncovered.

She giggled.

"Hey," he said, "what are you doing?"

"Posing for you."

"You should be asleep."

"Nobody else thinks that I have a beautiful profile." In the light of the street lamps her eyes had become very dark, magical. "I've tried to imagine what life would be without you."

"Peaceful and quiet," he said.

"Yes, that too. And it would be ordinary, and I would be a very ordinary woman, not the exciting, temperamental, artistic creature you've made me into." She was trying to laugh. "I am even a better teacher now. Can you understand it? I am better at home! Can you understand it in terms of sin?"

"No." He gently kissed her hair. "Don't cry."

"I am not crying. You are much more of a crier than I am."

"I wish we could be like little children," he said.

"I wasn't happy as a little girl."

"We could just be walking around holding hands, and nobody would think twice about it."

"And you wouldn't need to go to bed with me," she said. A car went around the traffic circle with squealing tires; then it was quiet again.

"I was trying to figure it out," he said. "Is it because I am a man or because I want to be a part of you?"

"Why did you put your hand over my face?"

"You were breathing so quietly that I was afraid. I wanted to make sure."

"Oh, you," she said. "Come lie down beside me." One of the church clocks boomed out. The others took up the sound.

*   *   *

He woke up just as the clock stopped bonging. It was three o'clock. In the silence he could hear a dripping faucet count down the seconds. He reached out his hand over her face. Her breath came reassuringly in warm little puffs, suffusing him with love that he could hardly contain, that needed Wagnerian sounds, sounds without words, a speaking in tongues beyond the ability of any language. And his mind cried out to God, defying conventions about when to pray and when not to pray, when to give thanks and when to refrain.

"I don't want you to think," she mumbled, "that Tony isn't a kind man." She touched his hand and turned on her side.

"I never did," he said. She went on sleeping, and he thought how all good things came from God in any situation and that the pain he felt and that she would have called punishment was self-inflicted. He wanted to hibernate, bearlike, to wake up to numbness, to a dull, passionless, limited life without pain. Twenty miles away was Dover and the English Channel and, just across it, France, where he would have hardly had an accent. They could have lived in an old peasant cottage, painting and talking, and on the streets they could have walked hand in hand, even in daylight. Dover was only twenty miles away, but she slept trustingly beside him, and so it might as well have been the distance to the sun. The money he had could have lasted six months, by which time ... by which time he would be frantically lining up subjects for pastel portraits, since nobody would buy his oils, which underlined the fact that Tony the bank manager, her husband, was younger than he was, had a degree from Cambridge, and had made it possible for her to move out of her parents' row house into a Victorian mansion on a rise. And Tony was nice and he looked like the man in the Jaguar ad.

He slid out of the bed, moving slowly like a man with a stomach wound, holding himself together with his arms. He found the newspaper under the chair. The bathroom door was ajar with the light left on, and he remembered how only last night he had thought of the children they would have and that they would always travel with them, and that in strange places he would always keep a door ajar with a light behind it for their mother's sake as well.

He opened the paper to find the time for an early communion. His tears falling on the open pages made a strange, hollow sound.

*   *   *

Over the murmured words he could hear the priest's vestments flap like flags in a breeze. He smelled the wine and the dusty carpets, kneeling there at the altar rail with eyes closed, floating, weightless. He was glad that he was a foreigner and a stranger, knowing that nobody would take any notice of him and that would spare him a worse guilt for coming here among them. He knew the truth about himself: he was a fallen man who could not stay away. Without Christ he had no identity, no name, no country, no existence, no life.

He was kneeling with his torso swaying in tiny circular motions, a wounded tree the moment before crashing down — waiting. He was waiting for another miracle. With shaking hands he reached out and touched the bottom of the cup.

Vladimir's Kitchen

S ensing light, the birds in the rookery awoke. The sky had become a delicate pale green that opened up, fanlike, metamorphosing into a red disk that mirrored itself in the lake, glorious and unearthly. A heron croaked, a single cello tuning up amidst an orchestra of woodwinds. The man sitting by the lake stood up and began to walk toward a duplex built next to a clump of cabbage palms on top of a rise.

There were five cement-block buildings at the Center: a duplex for the trainees (he was the only one), a building that a sign declared was the LIBRARY but which housed field hampers instead of books, and, closer to the lake, three large houses. The first was occupied by the coordinator, a graduate student of sociology who was writing a master's thesis on co-ops in rural settings, and the second by the director, a seminary graduate who wasn't certain that he wanted to be a pastor after all. The third house, almost on the lake, belonged to Dr. Biggs, a retired agricultural missionary. He had built the house himself, using live trees as uprights.

The Christian Service Training Center had officially been opened in the final year of President Truman's last term. On eight hundred acres, it was located fifteen miles outside Lime, Florida (pop. 1,012), between Grantham Swamp and Lake Knox. Because of the location's subtropical climate, it was the perfect place to study agriculture useful to people living in rural poverty in Latin America and the southern portions of the United States. The trainees were to be taught by retired missionaries with the Bible in one hand and President Truman's Point IV proposal in the other.

He first heard about the Center during a ten-minute traffic jam on a bridge between Camden, New Jersey, and Philadelphia. The sermon, in Russian, was on the theme of "Go ye therefore . . ." given by a fellow prism-grinder called Vladimir. The sermon lasted exactly five minutes because, as soon as they were off the bridge, Vladimir stopped talking. Rush-hour traffic had always made Vladimir nervous, especially as it funneled into his narrow street, bordered by soot-gray, five-storied houses, a canyon closing in misery and despair. In each block there were boarded-up shops and people leaning against them as if caught in a chemical process that transformed and fused two alien elements into a new permanent entity. Vladimir's apartment house was protected by a curbside honor guard of khaki garbage cans.

"Come up, Andre, and visit," Vladimir said. "I have some thick bacon and a bottle of vodka."

"Thank you. I will." He too liked to eat cured, uncooked bacon despite his wife's warnings about trichinosis. Meg was an American. He estimated that before coming to America he had been eating smoked, uncooked bacon for at least fifteen years and had never had any stomach complaints other than hunger pains.

He often drove Vladimir home from work, but he had never been invited in before. They were friends in spite of the twenty years' difference in their ages. Their friendship was mostly due to the fact that though he could speak only limited Russian with Vladimir, neither of them could talk baseball with the others in the shop. They worked for a Quaker optical company that produced periscopes for tanks.

The building's front door was bleached to the color of chocolate left too long in a refrigerator. The stairs were wet from washing that did not clean anything, and gave off an odor that was somehow European, an odor made up of the wet sacking used in the scrubbing, cat urine, and poverty.

Vladimir's apartment was on the top floor. His front door wasn't locked.

"Come," Vladimir said in Russian. "Come."

They entered the hallway. The walls were painted creamy white, and the parquet floor shone with the mellowness of spread honey. The smell of furniture polish and floor wax mingled with the smell of port. The quietness and peace seemed otherworldly after the rush-hour traffic on the streets. He followed Vladimir toward a tall, winged door, remembering the crossing from Europe, the clean cabins and dining rooms, the calls to the "sittings" and the food that seemed to come to their table in an endless stream that promised to fill him forever, yet by the next meal he was starving again with the hunger of a colicky baby. Meg had said that his hunger was at least partly psychological.

The right-hand side of the winged door was open. He looked in, forgetting all about the psychology of hunger, even forgetting Meg, nine months pregnant now.

The room — it must have been a studio once — was divided by an icon screen hung with small oval paintings in brilliant reds, blues, browns, whites, and gold, gold everywhere on the portrait of the Savior, of Mary and Joseph, of St. Michael. He recognized them in the way he had recognized old pictures in the family albums, oval sepia photographs of his great-grandmothers and great-grandfathers who had died long before he was born. The light coming through the window set in the pitched ceiling was harsh, the frozen, colorless light of a black-and-white glossy taken with a flash. Only below the sanctuary lamp was there any warmth. Vladimir was kneeling under the lamp with his face turned toward the screen.

*   *   *

He was home by seven-thirty. Six hours later Lee was born at the University of Pennsylvania medical school. On the way to the hospital, wanting to distract Meg, he had told her about Vladimir's church.

Two weeks later they had made an appointment with Mr. Renshaw, the philanthropist developer connected with the Christian Service Training Center, and when Lee was three weeks old they started on their trek to Florida.

*   *   *

By the time he reached the LIBRARY and smelled the ghost of the onion crop that had been dried there earlier in the year, it was fully morning. The sun that by August would become an enemy was a welcome touch on his back. It was April.

The screen door on the south side of the duplex opened, then slapped shut. He could see Meg, with Lee riding on her hip, looking toward the lake, and he thought of all the centuries of paintings and carvings of the Madonna and the Child, attempting to recapture this sense of the holy.

"Andre," Meg shouted, "breakfast." She was coming toward him. "You didn't come to bed last night."

"I stayed outside after Dr. Biggs finished talking to me. I needed to think," he said, knowing that the truth was he wanted to quarantine himself, as if the carrier of bad news equaled the carrier of some dread disease.

"Whenever you say you need to think, we are all in trouble," Meg said. She handed Lee to him. He held her to himself, smelling her clean American baby smell, remembering that before Lee was born he always thought that babies would smell the same as puppies, like bologna. There was no scientific explanation for puppies smelling like bologna, but they did. When he was a little boy, his sister, two years older, used to explain the inexplicable with the word *because*. His sister was dead now. Killed. Because.

"Dr. Biggs found out that all the deeds to the Center lands are in Mr. Renshaw's name."

"Well, that's not something to worry about, is it?" Meg said. They entered the duplex. The screen door slapped shut behind them. There were pancakes for breakfast. The smell of maple syrup made the day seem a Sunday. It was Good Friday.

"Mr. Renshaw had two previous projects, one in New York State, the other in Arizona. They both folded."

"That doesn't mean that this project will fold, does it?" Meg took Lee from him and put her on the cement floor. She crawled to the screen door.

"You don't understand, Meg. The projects died because Mr. Renshaw killed them. He stopped paying the staff and the bills; then when everybody had left, he turned the projects into housing estates." He poured syrup on his pancakes. "We haven't been paid this month, Meg."

At the screen door Lee was waving her arms and laughing in her high, tiny girl's voice. A cat with its tail extended straight up glided back and forth in front of the door like a trolley bus.

*   *   *

He left the house at twenty to eight, as he had done every weekday morning for the past five months, to walk down to the director's house for his daily work assignment, thinking that he was not much different from the countless men on countless town squares who waited to be hired as day laborers. Most of the time he worked alone stretching fences or putting in culverts, just to take them up the next day because Rick Hartley, the director, or Joe Coogler, the coordinator, or Mr. Renshaw, who visited the Center at least twice a month, changed his mind. Walking by the LIBRARY, he was thinking that only a few months ago, he was certain of the presence of God. He remembered Vladimir's kitchen, the straight, wooden chairs and the two of them sitting at a pine table, eating bacon rubbed with paprika and drinking vodka from small glasses, overwhelmed by God's love. It didn't seem incongruous then to see Vladimir's glowing, happy face, even knowing that Vladimir's father had been turned into an ice sculpture by the Bolsheviks.

He passed an open shed that was to be the DAIRY but had ended up like the LIBRARY, full of field hampers. Nothing was what it seemed. The Center was a fun house in an amusement park. Look at the philanthropist: now you see him, now you don't. And here is the missionary trainee walking down a narrow sand path made in five months of trudging for the love of God. Only that wasn't true, either. He had come to the Center more from fear than love, fear that made him sweat, made his heart beat with the sound of a pile driver, fear that came close to exploding his head. He had come to make a deal that would stop the picture in his mind, to erase that one still, that single frame of his sister with her arms out, a lone, silent cross pinned against a wall, pinned there by the back of a truck with its motor racing. That was the only sound, the motor racing. Then the olive-green truck moved forward; the blue-epauletted soldiers climbed aboard and drove away. When he could make himself move, it was too late. He had thought then that his coming out of the hiding place earlier wouldn't have helped her, that they would just have killed him too. But a few hours later, when the thought of pain didn't overwhelm him, he began to wonder why he was alive.

The large cement foundation he passed was the DORMITORY. Mr. Renshaw's dark green Buick was parked in front of the director's house. He went around the DORMITORY so that he wouldn't have to walk in front of the house with all of them in the living room. He knocked on the kitchen door as always, and Rick, as always, opened it.

"Hi," Rick said. "Come into the living room. Mr. Renshaw is here."

"Thank you." Usually he got his work orders in the kitchen. He wondered if he would have the courage to ask Mr. Renshaw for his wages — Mr. Renshaw called it a stipend — and decided that he would just wait for Mr. Renshaw to bring it up.

"Good morning, Andre." Mr. Renshaw smiled and moved his arm in greeting. It reminded him of the early, silent newsreels of the trooping of the colors, where a king took the salute, the arm flashing jerkily up and down, giving the impression not so much of a salute but of a man touching his head in pain.

"Morning, Sir."

"How are Meg and the little one?"

"Fine, thank you."

"I called this meeting with Joe and Rick," Mr. Renshaw said, clearing his throat, "and you too, of course . . . to tell you all that we must tighten our belts. Retrenching is in order. Unfortunately for you, Andre, the Center can survive the absence of a trainee, but not the absence of the director or the coordinator. This isn't a reflection on your performance, Andre, I assure you. We simply haven't got the money." Mr. Renshaw smiled again.

"I understand." He didn't feel anything. It was much like the first time he was wounded — a stinging sensation in the back of his leg as if somebody had slapped it. He had only realized that he was wounded when the blood started sloshing in his boot. It happened fifty kilometers from Kiev. Three thousand kilometers from his home in Budapest. He remembered the snow and the crows sitting on the skeletons of the houses. He had never found out the name of the dead village.

"I am sorry," Joe Coogler said. He was blushing. Rick Hartley didn't say anything.

*   *   *

The screen door slapped shut behind him. Meg's note was propped against a jar filled with wildflowers. She'd taken Lee to her routine doctor's appointment. He loved her handwriting. It was a part of her, like her hands or hair or the way she walked.

There were warnings in the Book of Common Prayer against inordinate affection, but he never thought they applied to him. He believed that if the allotted time was short, it needed inordinate love. He didn't expect to live long. His father had died young of a shrapnel wound, and he himself was now older than his sister. He had overtaken her. Two weeks ago he was asked to give a talk in a Negro church in Babson Park behind the groves. On the way home he was shot at.

He turned on the radio. A man with an exaggerated bass voice was saying, "AND, THEY ARE MILD." Then the program in progress came back on. The discussion centered on a man called Troy McCann, who had been executed for murder on Monday. What was unfair, one of the panelists said, was the waiting on death row, the prolongation of agony by the attorneys. By the time the punishment was meted out, the general public couldn't recall either the crime or the victim. Another panelist thought it was most barbaric to make people walk to the electric chair, to make them walk to their own deaths.

He turned off the radio and went outside. The sky was cloudless, the blue of larkspur. Down near the lake stood a tall, dead pine. The lower portion of it had turned into a smooth, white column resembling a memorial to some forgotten cause. The top part, with its dark, dead branches, reached out like arms. The sky created a niche for the dead pine, a blue niche that separated it from all the green living trees. It stood alone, a cross, waiting.

Before becoming a prism grinder in Camden, he had been an art model, hanging from crosses for three dollars an hour. The first few minutes never hurt much, but soon he wasn't able to hold up his head, and the ticking of the timer filled him with a paranoia of the ugliest kind that silently accused all of them in the studio of cheating, of setting the timer for forty minutes instead of the twenty-five they had agreed on. He remembered trying to hold his breath to rest his back muscles, but then the next breath hurt even more, and his heart beat so loudly that it drowned out the timer. He could feel the semicircle of artists watching him. They were all dressed. He, in his homemade loincloth, was almost naked. He hated them.

Then somebody would shout "Rest!" but he couldn't rest till they removed the two-by-four, the top part of the cross.

"Walk around," somebody would say, and he would walk around, hating them even more because the five-minute break was almost over. The pain was real. There was nothing symbolic in it even if they didn't use nails.

A breeze sprang up. The crowns of the trees moved from side to side — a group of mourners in their lamentation. The grass undulated in gentle waves, lapping toward where he was standing thinking of Jesus trudging up the hill, moving his beaten body step by step closer to the final torture, where the pain in his hands and feet would become suffocation and where nobody would shout "Rest!" It didn't really matter that the Christian Service Training Center would be turned into a housing development or that he was out of a job. He knew beyond any dogma or theological explanation that Jesus was trudging up the hill to die for him. This was the fellow guest who had come to Vladimir's kitchen.

"My Lord," he said. He lay down with his face touching the sand and wondered how he could contain the love that filled him.

Lazarus

It was cold with the damp, bone-chilling cold of Florida winter days.
It never lasted longer than two or three days at a time, but on days
like those the sun would be dying, hidden behind a dirty white blanket.
The wind was blowing, making the cedars whistle, rattling the leafless
branches of trees and the remains of the corn.

The corn stood behind the house next to the vegetable garden,
close enough for the water hose to reach. It was a frame house with
peeling white paint, a rusting tin roof, and a front porch worn gray by
the sun and rain. The house was, along its side from front to back, the
image of a Primitive Baptist church; yet the front, with its Neo-Gothic
roof and Victorian stained glass, suggested an Episcopal one. Before
being planted among the trees on a forty-acre farm, it had been an an-
tique shop in town.

The house had been rented to a family of four. Some of the neighbors thought that the family had come from England, others that they
came from South Carolina. But it didn't really matter, since the closest
neighbors lived a mile and a half away and were not inclined to visit.
They saw the children at the side of the road waiting for the school bus
every school day, and they glimpsed the wife driving to work. She was
a small woman with auburn hair and a sweet face. The children must
have taken after her. The husband was big. He had black hair, brown

eyes, and high cheekbones. He didn't go to work anywhere as far as anyone knew. He did a little dirt farming and bought the groceries. He had an accent, but nobody knew what kind since it wasn't Cuban.

Once when he was at the grocery store and was asked about his nationality he said, "I am an American," and scowled.

Now he was in the kitchen, waiting for the water to boil so that he could make tea for his daughter, Sibet, who was home with a sore throat. He shouldn't have been glad, but he was. As a tiny girl she had followed him around like a puppy dog, and he loved her with a love that had overwhelmed him since he first saw her. The nurse had brought her out from behind a glass wall, and he had asked to hold her. Holding her in his arms, looking at her perfection, he lifted her to thank God. The nurse took her away.

The kettle began to whistle. He made tea, enjoying the steam warming his face. The only heat in the house came from the kerosene stove in the alcove populated by two dogs, between the bathroom and the children's bedroom.

"Here is your tea, Sibet," he said.

"Thank you, Daddy." She was nine years old with a lovely nose, green-gray eyes, and dark brown hair in pigtails. The room was painted sky blue, which made it seem filled with light. One window looked out on the desolation of the vegetable garden.

"How is your throat?"

"Much better."

"Shall we talk about our donkey cart or the four ponies that will pull our little stagecoach? . . . Twenty-five cents a ride."

"I think Johnny should be the driver, and you and I will be the bandits who hold up the stage," she said. "Of course we just pretend holding it up."

"Of course."

They talked realistically about feed prices and the likely stage-coach passengers and names of the ponies, who were all pinto. By eleven-thirty the stagecoach route was extended to cover all the schools in town, and the business provided income to build a seventy-five-foot schooner, the *Elisabeth*. It was painted the same blue as the room and had red sails like the Thames coal barges. After six weeks of uneventful crossing (*no, no*, the girl said, *we saw porpoises dancing*), they glimpsed the Devon coast and were guided in by the blinking light that stood on Jubilee to direct the fishermen of Beer.

"The light is at the bottom of Jubilee next to the men's room, Daddy."

"You are right. . . . Should we run the boat up on the shingle?" He was surprised that he was thinking seriously about the landing. The fishermen used to nose into shore, jump out, attach the cable, get the rollers under while the winch was slowly pulling up the boat. But would that be possible with a seventy-five-foot schooner?

"I can smell it," the girl said, happily hugging her knees. So could he. The odor of drying seaweed, nets, and lobster pots; the salty wind that with the changing of direction became a fish-and-chips concentrate; the pine smells and the kale, too, that came down from the surrounding fields.

"Where we picked mushrooms," the girl said.

The fields divided by hedges were a huge eiderdown with deep green dominating the pattern. Seagulls circled the church steeple, crying a harsh, heartbreaking, homesick cry, to be answered by a flock of sheep grazing by Castle Rocks. Their mouths were full of dry winter grass, yet they sounded as if it were cotton wool. Above all, or perhaps around it all, was a rhythmic panting like an engine waiting at a railway station — the sea rolling the shingle.

"You left out the two little lambs, Daddy."

"To tell it, it has to be winter." He looked out of the window. The walnut tree was a stark, gray Vishnu against a stark, gray sky. When the wind blew hard, the Spanish moss swung out almost horizontal, like acrobats on a flying trapeze.

"And we need snow." There was another problem. "And Johnny should be along too."

"This time he won't be with us when we meet the two little lambs because he is in school," the girl said. The man marveled how easy it was for the child to move back into the past and alter it so that the present would fit it. He saw the day too, but for him nothing had changed: snow on the ground and piled up high on the hedges, Grandfather in his gray-tweed shooting cape, walking straight-backed, his curly white hair uncovered, followed by Freya the collie, John, Sibet, and himself bringing up the rear. The gulls were swooping and diving, wisps of cloud against the church steeple. He remembered and felt the affection they had for each other, and he thought that if needed he would die for them, knowing that the proof he used was absurd, yet it could not be helped. And testing, testing, he again stood before the wall, facing the alien soldiers and their guns, letting the horror wash over him to make sure that if he must, he could do it. Then without any preliminaries he was in the oddly shaped drawing room. The sun rays touching the curtains turned into pink splotches on the wall opposite. There were flowers in the marble fireplace. Grandfather sat next to them on a low chair.

"Where there is a spark of love, there is a spark of spiritual life," he said. Outside the gulls were crying.

"Daddy," the girl said, "you still didn't tell it." And because the man was lost in thought, she told it herself. "Grandfather stays behind so that Freya should not scare the sheep, and you and Sibet go down toward the flock of sheep, and two little lambs come jumping and skipping toward the little girl. . . . Can you see it, Daddy?"

"You put your arms around them," he said, noticing that her face crumpled. "What's the matter?"

"My head hurts," she said, lying down. He brought two aspirin and a glass of water.

"This is pink children's aspirin."

The girl choked on the second aspirin but in the end got it down. "They were not cuddly, and they felt damp and oily and stuck together. The wool wasn't soft the way it looked." She began to cry.

"Why didn't you tell us if it mattered so much?"

"I didn't want Johnny to know. He was such a sweet little boy." She cried in earnest now.

"He still is, starting second grade." He touched her forehead. "You have a fever, and that is why you feel bad. I'll go outside with the dogs and let you sleep awhile."

As soon as the dogs heard "outside" and "dogs," their tails beat on the kerosene stove. He went to get his gun, thinking that as the world judged he was a failure because he couldn't get a paying job, and work itself was not honored so that his farming counted for nothing, yet he was happy and felt whole. His wife, his children, his dogs loved him; the soil in their garden was rich; and there was always enough to eat.

He reached the gun rack, and the next instant there was an illumination. It could not be called anything else. What he saw was a box very much like the boxes he had seen in the National Gallery at Trafalgar Square, boxes fabricated by seventeenth-century Dutch artists, containing different rooms, some with their owners in them, all done in perfect scale. His own box was open at the back, and he was looking toward the nave, where four people were kneeling. He recognized himself and his wife and children. The dogs were there too, their ears softly relaxed, their forepaws piously crossed. Then he looked at the great light on the altar, a golden light, and his heart began to beat with the slow booming of bells just brought into motion. Instead of the chalice and the ciborium, he saw the Lord standing there, surrounded by this curious light that made him finally understand the word *Glory,* and he longed with an infinitely sad longing to touch His feet. He reached out, feeling tears well up.

Outside it was bleak, the damp cold making him shiver. The dogs ran through the pecan grove. Gusts of wind tore at the Spanish moss; then he was through the grove and into an old field. It was there that the dogs struck, their voices high, excited, going toward the swamp, disappearing in it, then coming back. He saw them coming toward him, but there was no rabbit in front of them. Not far from him they stopped, sheepishly looking from him to a clump of grass. He couldn't read the dogs at all. Then he saw them too and, breaking the gun open, pocketed the shells. The three little rabbits kept perfectly still. Looking at them close up was an affirmation of Dürer's mastery. They were gray-brown-white in color. One had dark fur inside its ears. They looked soft.

A second later he scooped up the rabbits and put them into the front pocket of his sweatshirt, knowing that now the mother would never come back for them but not thinking of this. He thought of his daughter. The rabbits felt soft, like butterflies palpitating on yellow flowers.

*   *   *

The man was driving back from town with the groceries and a bagful of slightly spoiled greens. The greens were for the rabbits, which had survived feedings with dolls' baby bottles and the dogs' sanitary lickings, and were now ready to be turned loose.

The car turned off Highway 441 onto a side road, passed a log house with a TV aerial, a Quonset hut seemingly filled with baying hounds, then Sunshine Stables, and, turning left by a pond covered with duckweed, drove up to the house. Seeing it, the dog hanging over his shoulder began to lick his face. The other one lying on the back seat sat up, ready to leave the car. They were home.

He carried the grocery bags into the kitchen — vegetables into the icebox, staples into the larder — then he was ready with a handful of lettuce. The rabbits lived in a basket in the alcove. They were not in their basket, but that was all right; jumping out of the basket was a sign of progress. He found two of them under his son's bed and put them back into the basket. Their noses wrinkled as they nibbled the lettuce.

After a while the man stopped watching and decided to get the third rabbit, the one with the dark fur inside its ears.

By the time he searched the bathroom, feeling the cracked linoleum against his face as he peered under the tub, it ceased to be a routine getting the rabbits back into the basket. The rabbit with the black fur inside its ears was definitely lost.

He went outside to get help from the dogs, but they had gone hunting on their own. Back again in the house, he was assailed by nameless fears starting in his body that froze like a bird dog coming up on a covey. He knew that this was ridiculous, thinking of the real horrors cataloged and presented in neat Pablum jars for five minutes of every hour in the ceaseless litany of a fallen world. He was looking only for a lost rabbit. Then he noticed the back door of the kitchen was ajar, and there was new hope; the back porch was screened in, and its door was always closed.

The floorboard creaked under his feet. He looked down. The rabbit was lying on its side, stretched out, rigor mortis already set in.

"God," he said aloud. "God." The rabbit in his hands felt like a wet glove frozen dry. He thought of his children, whom he wanted to shield but could not, remembering their faces when they were told that their only living grandfather was dead.

Tomorrow was Saturday, and the whole family would have taken the rabbits to Oleno State Park, where there was no hunting, and turned them loose. Just one more day. Seeing their joy that had never been — the rabbits disappearing into the woods, the children jumping up and down, and he and his wife standing together watching all this in the same way they read poetry together — he moaned.

He should have gone outside to get a shovel, but instead he went inside to the alcove. The two rabbits were in their basket on a table next to the kerosene stove. There was a smaller basket on the table, and he put the dead rabbit in it. With God everything is possible, he thought, not believing it. He stood there, not feeling or thinking anymore. Then he screamed. The dead rabbit had jumped at his chest. He was holding it in his hands now, away from himself, feeling a revulsion he had not felt with the dead body, and put the dark-eared rabbit with the others. He knelt ponderously, his body almost bent to the floorboard, as if heavy weights were pushing down on his shoulders. His lips said thank you, but he was thinking that he was an ordinary man who forgave himself too much for too many things, a man who hated injustice so much that in turn he was unjust himself. He had asked, not expecting an answer, and he had been answered. He had seen his own Lazarus. It was unbearable.

*   *   *

On Saturday it was sunny, and the river glinted as they walked over the suspension bridge. There were a lot of people at Oleno. Families were cooking hot dogs and hamburgers, the smoke of their fires going up straight toward the sky. There were young people everywhere and even some northern visitors braving the river. His children carried the basket on the bridge, but once they were over he asked them for it. He lifted the kitchen cloth, looking at the rabbits. They all seemed to have black fur inside their ears. He couldn't tell them apart.

He walked to the edge of the woods and gently dumped them out of the basket. His children began jumping up and down. He stood beside his wife, watching the rabbits disappear into the woods.

A Slow, Soft River

The girl was driving the car up the slope, bouncing over the ruts gouged out by the runoff; then, stopping a second, she waved. The man and the boy didn't look up from loading supplies in an old wooden boat half floating on the Itchetucknee. The river was cold and clear and smelled of the fish that swam close to the bridge, their heads pointing upstream. They were silver or black, nothing in between, with tails going like slow metronomes.

The girl turned onto the highway. When the man heard the car crossing the highway bridge, he lifted his hand and wiggled his fingers in farewell. The boy waded into the river. Hunching over the transom with the outboard, he looked like a stork fishing.

By next year, the man thought, he'll be taller than I am. The boy was sixteen and he, forty-five.

"Daddy," the boy said, straightening up, "we are ready to leave now."

"Sam," the man called. "Sam."

From under the bridge a big, gaunt, black and tan hound sauntered down to the boat. He had a false joint in his hip that made him drag his right hind leg. He came to the man and put his muzzle in his hand.

"Samuel," the man said. He felt love rising in him like a great shout that spread over the giant water oaks, the face of his daughter in the car framed by dark hair, her emerald eyes smiling good-bye, the wind on the pale green sea of the river with its island-pools of blue, his tall, strong son; and Sam. Sam, who had been found two years ago in a Georgia swamp on the verge of death. He lifted his arms as if he wanted to breathe in the blueness of the sky.

"Praise the Lord," the boy said matter-of-factly. "Get in, Daddy."

"Do you feel it too?" The man was astonished, as if the boy had suddenly spoken in Chinese.

"I don't know why I shouldn't. I'm normal."

They floated under the highway bridge, then shot through the culvert under the railroad tracks. There were some houses on the left bank, but nobody in them. The river turned and widened. A congregation of ducks bobbed on the ripples. They were white ducks with one blue-wing teal in the midst of them. Out of sight a heron sounded deep bass. The ducks tuned up. Then, as if the conductor had come in, there was a sudden silence. Sam stood up in the boat and, lifting his head, bayed.

"That was an otter," the boy said. Some turtles plopped into the water, one after the other. Sam lay down again.

"I feel the same as when I listen to Bach," the man said. "I am lifted up, I am soaring, and I am almost bursting with joy. . . . But it is all orderly."

"You can't orderly-burst-with-joy," the boy said.

"We better crank up." The man was looking ahead where the Itchetucknee ran into the Santa Fe. There was a large object caught in the turbulence, coming up and going under again like a drowning man.

The engine started with a shriek; then the boy slowed it down to a pleasant purr. They went around the obstacle. Close up it was only a tree trunk that turned with a nice, even speed. A roller in a well-oiled machine.

The Santa Fe was wider and darker and so swollen that it hardly moved between the banks of moss-covered trees. The boy speeded up. Two long waves left behind by the boat rushed the banks like charging cavalry, then broke up into shiny fragments among the tree trunks. Dry land was nowhere in sight. The man turned his head to the other side. A new charge just broke among the trees, flashing here and there like pieces of broken mirror. Without warning he saw his friend Stefan on the hospital bed as he had been the last six weeks, breathing through a hole in his neck, his chest heaving, his eyes half closed. Then the sun came out, illuminating the spaces among the trees. The green patent-leather leaves of a huge magnolia reflected the light upward.

A garment of praise for the spirit of heaviness, he thought.

The boat changed direction, then got back on course. The boy had just finished taking off his shirt.

"Aren't you cold?"

"I wouldn't have taken it off if I were," the boy said.

"Vanity," the man said. "You want to get tanned; somebody else wants to bleach out. It's all vanity."

"If we all have it, you must have it too, Daddy."

"I have it moderately. On some Sundays when it is cold enough to wear my suit which I got to go to England in, I think, aha, not bad at all, but your mother will say, 'It's all right if you don't put on any more weight.' And I quit saying 'aha' till next winter."

"I remember when you bought that suit. I was five years old."

"That can't be."

"It was when I was starting school in England."

"And I am still not famous," the man said, "but at least I can get into my old suit."

"You look great in it, Daddy."

The man accepted this with a slight bow. He remembered how he stood in the door of the intensive-care unit, not knowing if he should go in, conscious of his good suit and the nurses who were looking at him. But it didn't last long, this male pride, because he saw Stefan and understood that the rhythmic clicking he heard came from a green plastic pump attached to a hole in Stefan's neck. Stefan was pale, his unseeing eyes half open. For a crazy moment he had almost expected Stefan to ask him to have something to eat or to drink wine. He always did. But there was nothing other than the sudden, awful silence of the pump. He was holding his own breath, wanting to share the pain; then the pump started, and Stefan's chest expanded. The rhythm of the pump was back for a while; then it stopped again. He had reached out and laid his hands on Stefan's head.

"Do you want to fish?" the boy was shouting over the noise of the outboard. "Now that the sun is out I can see the fish." He cut back the engine.

"They prophesied rain," the man said, "but it doesn't look like it. I'll just sit and watch you fish."

They anchored under a large oak. The boy cast, the bait falling like a meteor plopped into the river. Sam checked the sound. The boy reeled in and cast out again. Some ducks came in over the trees and settled on the Santa Fe.

"It's good to be away from the world," the man said.

"This is the world, Daddy." The boy reeled in again.

"I am glad that at least Sam can't talk back," the man said. "I am talking about this place where we can see and smell the sun."

"Yes," the boy said.

"I think it's all right for us to be here."

"Why wouldn't it be all right? We can't do anything for Stefan except pray."

"Even so, I saw Stefan at the nursing home and you didn't. There is no pump beside his bed now, and that awful clicking is gone, but in a way it is worse. He struggles for each breath, and when I squeezed his hand there was nothing. In the hospital at least he squeezed back, and I always thought of it as Stefan in a sunken submarine answering my knock, saying, 'I am here, I am here, I can hear you.'"

"I looked it up," the boy said, putting on his shirt. "The veins contract first to prevent too much bleeding, but if they don't relax after a certain time, that part of the brain dies."

"Stefan was just lying there sweating," the man said, not smelling the sun, the river, and the fishes anymore, "and his pillow showed the damp outline of his head."

"I don't want to think of him that way," the boy said. "I always see him playing golf, standing on that very green grass." He cast, the line flying out toward the other shore with a satisfying sound. The man saw Stefan, but he wasn't playing golf. He was sitting in his living room, in his dark green armchair next to a large candlestick, with papers strewn around him on the carpet. Just two hours before the stroke.

"No bother at all," Stefan said. *"While I read it, you eat something. And have some wine."*

"I have a nibble," the boy whispered. He leaned forward tensely, watching his line. "It's a bite, real heavy."

Play it, the man wanted to say, but he didn't say anything. The boy was a fisherman; he wasn't. He remembered his own fishing in the Danube with a cane pole and the dozens of fingerlings he pulled out from its olive-colored water. He also remembered his father's smile that said, This is all right for a little boy, but men, our kind of men, hunt.

"A fighter," the boy shouted, reeling in and letting out the line again. "A fighter." The fish leaped clear of the water, then went down, making the reel scream like an ambulance. "I am pulling him in now," the boy said. He turned the reel, his torso leaning forward in the attitude of a Protestant at prayer.

"I'll help you land it," the man said.

"I can manage, thank you." He stood up and lifted the fish into the boat. The fish — it was a bass — fell to the floorboard with a thud. The boy took out the hook. The bass kept on flapping on the board, then lay still. The man was watching its gills pumping in and out, in and out.

"Let's turn it loose," the man said.

"Why? It's a perfect eating size. It must be at least five pounds."

When the boy was younger, he cried easily. The look he gave now was a man's incredulous stare. I couldn't tell him, the man thought. Besides, it would be all wrong. Pagan. An exchange with the god of the river.

The fish flopped once, then lay still. Suddenly it lit up as if a light had been turned on inside it.

"It's beautiful," the boy said. "It gave a good fight."

*　　*　　*

By carefully navigating among the cypress knees and tree trunks, they reached the shore under a bluff. In the silence of the switched-off outboard, the tea-colored waves sounded like heavy breathing.

"I like to look down on the Suwannee," the man said. "This is how a flying heron sees it."

The boy laughed. "A two-hundred-pound heron. You would need a steel-reinforced king-size nest."

The bluff's floor was flat and covered with dry grass and the contorted trunks of live oaks. Sam checked out the place by circling around it. The man set up the tent. The boy chopped wood, built the fire, then neatly arranged his cooking tools on a stump.

"How do you feel about fish soup?" he asked.

"With plenty of paprika," the man said. He walked down to the edge of the bluff and looked down on the Suwannee. Its color alternated between royal blue and green with the edges saffron. There were no boats going in either direction. Some ducks dove, then bobbed back to the surface. Sam came to stand against the side of his knee.

"Sam thinks this is a good place," the man said. He saw Stefan's saffron-colored shoes that he still wore even after shaving off his guardsman mustache and returning to his more conservative look. "I might get a crew cut," Stefan had said. "That would make me avant-garde now." But he didn't. His hair was damp and matted on the pillow. "A nice full head of hair," the nurse had said.

"Do you want to taste the soup, Daddy?"

It tasted perfect, and he slurped another spoonful.

"Who is to put a price on the joy of sitting here tasting your fish soup?"

"Some rivers had to be dammed up because people needed electricity. You can't damn progress, Daddy."

"I don't. I wouldn't be here without it. I was pretty badly shot up in the war. It isn't that at all."

"We can eat now," the boy said.

"Anything for Sam?"

The boy gave the dog a few uncooked hot dogs. The man watched the dog. When Sam ran, he looked perfect. Only walking and sitting showed his crooked hip joint. We are both here, the man thought. It could have ended for Sam in that swamp in Georgia and for me at the border, under the barbed wire.

"Benedictus, benedicet."

"Deo gratias," the boy answered.

After washing up, the man climbed back up the bluff. He put the cooking utensils away and sat down on the blanket in front of the tent. For the last six years he and the boy had left on their annual boat trip on the Thursday before Easter. On Good Friday they would have a service of their own and be back at church on Easter Day. But this time it was different. He couldn't wait another day, and he needed the strength of his son. The boy was whole, while he was bruised and battered, only hoping to be made whole. The boy knew that with God everything was possible; he only hoped.

"John," the man said, "let's have our service today. It's because Stefan . . . we are out here, and he — "

"I thought about it," the boy said. He stepped into the tent, got the prayer book, and sat down on the blanket.

"You read," the man said. "I left my reading glasses at home." He loved to hear the boy read, and besides, his own accent made him uncomfortable knowing that it would ruin something precious. The boy opened the prayer book.

"Now before the feast of the passover, when Jesus knew that his hour was come that he should depart out of this world unto the Father, having loved his own which were in the world, he loved them unto the end — "

The man listened, already thinking of tomorrow, when He would be led to Pilate and shame and rejection and torment so that he, sitting here on a dog-smelly blanket, could be made clean and whole again.

" — For I have given you an example, that ye should do as I have done to you." The boy closed the prayer book. "Lord, we lift up our friend Stefan like those men who took the roof apart so that You could see their friend. You know what to do. We don't. Thank You."

"Amen," the man said, feeling peace carrying him along like a slow, soft river. He knew that he didn't have to worry about Stefan any-more.

The boy put away the prayer book in the tent and came back with a cigar.

"I didn't know that you were smoking. That cigar's at least six months old."

"I don't," the boy said. "Stefan taught me to blow smoke rings. They would float beautifully out here."

This time the man didn't ask the boy if he felt it too. He looked at his watch. It was four-thirty.

Just before dusk, the boy, who was fishing sitting in the tied-out boat, called him. There was a snake swimming across the river from the other side.

*   *   *

The rain began at noon Friday, and it was still raining when they pulled out the boat at Fanning Springs. The wood around the boat ramp smelled like mushrooms. There were cars crossing the battleship-gray bridge at long intervals, messengers from another civilization. In the pause the only sounds were the rain splashing on the Suwannee, the river itself, and Sam's running on the wet leaves.

The boy was stacking up the camping gear with an economy of movement. He had done this so many times that he could do it with his eyes closed. The man was standing facing the bridge, waiting. He was happy. The trip was accomplished, to be cherished and savored in detail and compared to other trips till next year, when another would be added. He was waiting for his wife to come with the car and boat trailer, waiting with the same gratefulness to catch a glimpse of her face as he had waited long ago in an English church. There was peace in this waiting, a healing where nothing of the bigger world intruded, so that when in time he would turn on the car radio he would not be crushed by the hate and despair.

"Here she is," he said. The car rumbled across the bridge, the empty trailer bouncing behind it. The trip was over. "John, go and back it down for her."

He watched them embrace; then the boy got in the car, turned it around, and backed it down. She was walking toward him with Sam, who had joined her. In his happiness he didn't notice the tightness of her face, only that she was glad to see him.

"You haven't changed," he said.

"Why would I change in two-and-a-half days?" She put her arms around him. "You smell like a wet dog."

They loaded the boat and the gear and were off. It began to rain harder, coming down in gray sheets. The bridge rumbled under them; then they were on the highway. The boy was talking, telling about the trip from the beginning — the way they shot through the culvert under the railroad bridge and about the flock of ducks with one blue-wing teal in the midst of them. When he came to the fish he caught, the man remembered Stefan.

"How is Stefan?" he asked, interrupting the boy. He wasn't worried about him. He asked almost out of politeness. Even when she touched his arm he wasn't prepared for anything.

"He is dead," she said.

He heard the boy say "no," and his own fist crashed down on the steering wheel. The pain in his hand was the only feeling he had in the general numbness until he began to think and anger filled him against himself, against the river, against Thursday, when at four-thirty he and the boy sat on a bluff hearing and feeling and trustingly celebrating like two madmen in the wine cellar of a bombed-out house. Then everything stopped. He drove on, peering through the windshield, noticing the curve in the road, an abandoned shack, a forlorn cow with her calf at her side. He marveled at himself that he could go on driving when life had lost all meaning, because if Stefan was dead, then God was dead also, or He never had been in the first place, and he had lived his own life for the past twelve years in a mental ward, hallucinating. There never had been a dialogue, a blessing and saving, a Body and Blood, and he was alone in an existential nightmare.

"There was no way I could contact you, and Jane wouldn't let me, anyway," she said. "The women were in the room praying when suddenly Stefan sighed and relaxed. He was gone. He died on Thursday at about four-thirty."

Relief came with a rush, and with it the accustomed and bearable seasons of joy and sadness all marching toward Glory that was and is and ever shall be.

"Forgive me," he said. He began to cry.

Waxworks

He was a tall man who expected to see people at his own eye level, which he thought to be the norm. Unseen, they would walk up to him, coming in under his chin. He should have known better. The same thing applied to tanks in battle. Anybody sitting undetected in front of a tank could blow it up easily, since the machine guns could be depressed just so much. The only defense was to sit up in the open turret with a submachine gun that could be held vertically and shoot anything that moved. The tank crew's motto was "Trust no one." Perhaps because at the time he was just out of school, he thought the motto had indications, sub specie aeternitatis, that he couldn't live with. Now he lived with a barely visible skin graft on his face.

"There's Grandmother." His son, who at the age of twenty-eight was an inch taller than himself, did not miss her in the wheelchair. He had met her in Budapest for the first time when he was fifteen. Perhaps it was that journey that made him decide later on to become a geographer. "She never changes."

"Why is she in a wheelchair? What's wrong with her?"

"Nothing, Daddy. She's eighty-three. That's a long walk from the plane."

He looked at his mother, a survivor of two world wars and two revolutions, a spirit of strength, a spirit that had held them together as a family in the forties after his father's death when the bombs started falling, and he didn't see an eighty-three-year-old grandmother in a wheelchair but an empress in a howdah, entering Miami International Airport in triumph. She was turning her head from side to side, and he knew that soon she would pronounce on all she saw, her brown eyes brilliant even behind the thick post-cataract glasses.

"Mother," he said, remembering the fifteen years when the ocean was an unbridgeable barrier between them tacked onto the unmovable mass of the Soviet Empire. "Mother," he said again, watching her lift her right hand as if in a benediction, but it was only a signal to the airline employee to stop so that she could stand up. "Mother," he called for the third time. She peered at him as if he were a painting, an abstract that needed close inspection, then reached up and touched his face with both hands.

*　　*　　*

Four hours out of Miami driving north, driving toward home, he again saw the autumn shades, leaves the color of cardinals' hats and the green-brown of dogwood leaves that were not a part of the South Florida landscape. Pools of water covered the low-lying pastures. There had been six hurricanes in the Caribbean that year, but not one of them had reached Florida. He still thought of hurricanes in terms of air raids, but his native son knew better: Florida needed two or three good hurricanes to fill its aquifers.

They had had a five-year drought. Not extreme, but enough to keep him awake at night, trying to figure out a way to afford an irrigation system for the pastures. Then he would dream of his parched fields, seeing the dusty blades of grass, pale-green, furled-up blades, and would hear his own footsteps sounding as if he were marching on snow on a long retreat. Then, in September, at the beginning of the month, it had rained for three days without a letup. It was enough to green up the fields and wash down the dusty trees so that now even the memory of the drought was gone. He saw reeds and rushes among the Spanish moss–garlanded cypress trees and remembered Isaiah's Highway of Holiness and felt his soul rise, shout for joy, joy that had become a song of thanksgiving for this day that brought his mother to America, for his son, who had stood beside him in the confusion of the airport and made him feel safe as only his own father could make a frightened little boy feel safe in a safe world long ago, when it seemed that grandparents, nannies, parents, brothers, and sisters lived forever; safe as before the war, war that killed his father and swept him into the Army to teach him that death and mutilation were usual human occurrences.

"I have never seen anything like this," his mother said. "They look like long-bearded, friendly uncles." The two of them sat in the back seat. She was looking at a small copse of Spanish moss–covered oaks. There were cows all over the pasture, black, brown, gray, beef cows of all breeds mixed together like thick blobs of paint on a large canvas that could be seen clearly only from a distance.

*   *   *

The exits and entrances to the highway were surrounded with service stations advertising their brand of gasoline on large, oblong signs held up by telescopic poles, as if demonstrators had lined both sides of the highway with their non-negotiable demands. There were more and more billboards planted in the pastures flanking Interstate 75, harbingers of the next town, showing giant oranges and motels that were equipped not only with posturepedic mattresses and air conditioning, but also with hundred-channel TVs. There were billboards advertising restaurants, souvenir shops, housing estates, and retirement communities.

"What does it mean, COZY ELEGANCE, Johnnyka?"

"Think of an elegant pair of slippers lined with sheepskin," he said, wanting to be the one who answered her questions.

"Don't confuse her," John said. "It doesn't mean anything, Grandmother. It's advertising rubbish."

"What is WAXWORKS, Johnnyka?"

"Something like Madame Tussaud's, Grandmother."

Local traffic entered Interstate 75 from both directions, cars accelerating at intervals like projectiles in a trapshoot.

"After they killed Agnes, I wanted a wax figure made of her to dress in her clothes. Just to sit with me in the same room. That was all. That wasn't so much to ask, was it?"

The town lay below the highway, flat and spread out. Cars were moving endlessly on its streets, ants on the march, searching for something elusive.

"No, Mother, that wasn't too much to ask." She was looking at him, and he thought: I must tell her. There is no forgiveness without confession.

*   *   *

At the age of sixteen he was going through a stage where he felt called upon to teach the villagers, "their" villagers, about hygiene, about not having the manure pile next to the kitchen door, about burning anything that was unclean, since fire was the cheapest, most available sanitation tool. His mother objected to Jozsef Maria being included in his reforming zeal. Jozsef Maria was the village's retarded pig herder. He thought his mother wasn't worried so much about his confusing Jozsef Maria as about his catching TB from Jozsef Maria's dying mother. When he wasn't playing the "young lord" of the village, he was training on his own to become an Olympic swimming champion. Every second day in the summer holidays he swam ten kilometers downstream and then walked back. On this day — it was a Wednesday — he heard the village bell and began to run. By the time he reached the stone cross at the entrance of the village, he saw the flames and people rushing toward the fire, shovels and buckets in hand. There was movement from both ends of the village. The bell stopped ringing. The fire wagon with the big barrel rumbled by, pulled by two plow horses. Some of the bigger children rushed past it, shouting to each other. Then he saw it. It was Jozsef Maria's house. He was running again, passing people, bumping into swinging buckets, pushing children out of the way, running faster and faster, wanting to be the one who would help him most, wanting to change from being a recipient of Jozsef Maria's boundless admiration and love into a giver of real help that would bring him into a give-and-take relationship he could understand. As he came closer to the house, all the bustling movement slowed down, forcing him to walk till he reached the wall of immobile people, his own mother amongst them, her driver standing beside her. No chains were formed to pass on the buckets of water. The buckets, hanging limp from their owners' hands, gleamed with an out-of-place splendor. The fire wagon stood by, unused, the horses neighing with fear. The driver, still on the seat, his mouth slightly open, his head bent back, watched the roof cave in. They all smelled the odor of burning flesh that floated back and forth between them and the flaming house, so that whenever it left their nostrils, they thought it was only their imagination and waited to be certain. Jozsef Maria was standing close to the house, beating out the flames escaped from his mother's pyre. He was smiling his vacant idiot's smile.

Watching Jozsef Maria, he didn't even notice the first stones. Feeling the sting, he touched the back of his head. He couldn't imagine that the wetness was his own blood or that he was being stoned by his own people. When he turned back and saw their faces, it was as if a huge, dirty avalanche was rolling down on him. Then his mother's driver fired the shotgun into the air. They always carried a shotgun in the boot of the Rolls.

A week later he was sent to Italy for the summer. His mother didn't blame him for the charred remains or for the fire that could have destroyed the village. He was simply treated as if the idiocy of Jozsef Maria had rubbed off on him. Jozsef Maria was sent to the Lipotmezo asylum in Budapest.

*   *   *

His mother stayed with them for a month. The first week of November he drove her to the Tampa airport. She was to fly to French Canada to visit an old school friend before returning to Budapest. He was glad the return flight left from Tampa. He wanted her to see the airport that was already in the twenty-first century, where robot cars moved passengers between terminals and gates, and where emotionless computer voices communicated with a nervous, rushing humankind. The hotels, restaurants, shops, movie houses, ice cream parlors, liquor stores, and automobile agencies were under one giant, air-conditioned roof, physically separated from the operational part of the airport. Landings and takeoffs could be observed through a glass panel that gave the impression of watching a silent movie where contemporary planes with their shark-shapes were substituted for the old, World War I planes that still carried the signs of the Wright brothers' bicycle shop. What could not be screened out was the ghost of all the reunions and partings. He remembered tears at the Budapest West Station at the beginning of each school term, watching their father and mother through the window of the second-class carriage. He would be standing next to his sister Agnes, who would get off the train first, to disappear till the end of the term, in the company of three or four similarly dressed girls and a large, penguin-colored nun. There were railway stations going to the Eastern Front; there were railway stations coming back, stations where people were rounded up, stations where they checked papers, and stations where money was as good as a proper passport. Each occupation zone had its own horror story, but there was one common, overriding tale, the archetype of all cautionary tales: DON'T BE CAUGHT IN THE RUSSIAN ZONE. YOU'LL END UP IN THE GULAG. Then there was the dockside at the Hook of Holland on his way to an English coalmine. The tears there were caused by the cold wind. It was a cold July, and he was down to a pair of pants and a shirt.

"Why don't you finish your breakfast," his mother said. The restaurant, in contrast with all the airport modernity, looked like what he imagined to be the inside of a cuckoo clock.

"I weigh two hundred pounds, Mother. I don't need to eat more."

"What is that in kilos?"

"I can't remember, but it's no skin and bones, I assure you." They laughed and she patted his hand.

"Never mind. You are a tall, big man. Two hundred pounds becomes you." She patted the top of his hand again. This was the time to tell her. Whatever her reaction, Meg and the children wouldn't have to witness it. It had begun with Agnes's letters, saying she wanted to do something about the political situation in Hungary. For her children's sake. Her doctor husband was in jail. He had left Budapest with a valid passport to present a paper in London. When he returned, the situation had worsened. There was more repression. Nobody was allowed to leave Hungary. He had been out visiting the West. Perhaps he had come back with anti-state instructions. He was sent to prison for five years.

"Would you like more coffee, Mother?"

"That is what you call this hot, brown water?"

"If you would like espresso, I'll order it."

In Florida he first worked for a large ranching concern whose system was to divide the land and the herd so that the individual hired hand would be responsible for his own portion. The system was based on the talents parable. His own responsibility was for two-hundred-fifty cows, mostly scrub, six Angus and six Brahman bulls, and four working quarter horses on twelve hundred acres, half of which was improved pasture. Their next-door neighbor, five miles away, ran his own orange grove besides being a real estate attorney. They became friends because they both liked the Pogo comic strip. The man was divorced and lonely and drove over three or four times a week to eat with them. They talked politics, and soon he was translating his sister's letters to read aloud. The man had been in World War II as a gunner on a B-29.

After he was wounded, he worked with the OSS. He could help Agnes do something about the Soviet occupation. That was how the contact was made. He almost forgot about it. Then two years later there was a large envelope with a Hungarian postmark in their mailbox, a big rural-route box that allowed room for catalog-order parcels. The box, a bit rusty, hunched on top of a fence post, a mile and a half from the house. The envelope, the only mail that day, was made of the crudest paper imaginable, the slivers of wood crusting the surface looking like squashed scorpions. He shivered like a horse shooing away flies. He felt exposed standing on their dirt road and began to walk toward the woods beside the pond that looked like green ice with a wooden bird on it. As he came closer, the bird, a blue heron, flapped its wings. It sounded like wind rushing through the woods. The green ice was gone.

In the envelope was a black-and-white photo of his sister held up by her outstretched arms against a wall. The blood in front of her over-alls looked black.

"Mother."

"I must take my pills." She opened a silver box he recognized as his great-uncle's snuffbox and counted out three pills. Then from a vial she took two more. She swallowed each one with a sip of water, counting all the while. After that she took a curiously shaped, japanned box from her handbag and counted out four more pills, breaking the fourth into halves. He remembered the box had sat next to the carved monkeys in a cabinet his mother called a "vitrine." He even remembered the smell of it.

Half an hour later he watched his mother walk through the metal detector. Once through, she turned and waved at him.

*   *   *

He expected a card from Montreal, where his mother was staying for a week. He wanted to see her handwriting, the beautiful, sharp, gothic letters that always alarmed him and at the same time filled him with hope, hope undefined until now: he wanted his mother's approval for all of them, for his wife and children, for their dogs and horses, for the farm, America, their lives. It had taken some doing to go from a ninety-dollar-a-month ranchhand with a cow, garden plot, house, and kerosene furnished, to this, their own three-bedroom, two-bath house with a fireplace and air-conditioning on fifty acres of rolling land. There was a time when he didn't have the credit to buy a $120 roping saddle needed to get a job with Lykes Brothers.

Two weeks before his mother's arrival he had bought a load of woodchips and had spent three days spreading it on the drive, around the flowerbeds, fruit trees, ornamentals. When he brought her home from the Miami airport and they turned onto the two-mile-long dirt road leading to their house, he could hardly wait for her to see the place. The minute his son stopped the car, he ran around and opened the door for her. She got out with some difficulty, holding on to his hand, looking around the sweep of the driveway generously covered with the rich, reddish-brown, wetted-down woodchips.

"What is this trash doing on your driveway, my son?"

She thought of their farm as a "tanya." She couldn't imagine that they chose to live here and not in town. A "tanya" in her youth was a settlement out in the steppes populated by poor peasants, shepherds, herdsmen, and bandits. But she approved of their church, the preaching, the singing, the liturgy, and most of all the people, who received her like a long-awaited relative. She approved of Meg, and of Sibet and John, perfect grandchildren even though they were still unmarried; she approved of Bailey, the Labrador the color of Bailey's Irish Whiskey, and of Samba, a large chestnut thoroughbred with blue ribbons in dressage and Three Day Events.

There was no card from his mother. At the end of November he tried telephoning her in Budapest. There was no answer. He tried phoning every day for five days; then his fear of telephones returned. He wrote a letter reminiscing about her visit. He started to imagine the letter she would write to him, could even see the blue envelope with the darker blue border and the oblong printed on the left side looking like a postal stamp with the logo LEGIPOSTA, underneath which the smaller letters declared "Par Avion." He could imagine her handwriting easily enough. He had seen it more often than he had seen the person of his mother. The salutation was always the same: "My sweet son."

The telegram came the second week of December. His mother had been dead for three weeks.

* * *

He went outside to be alone. The day was one of those incredible spring-like December days in Florida, with a sky the blue of Mary's color, the billowing, backlit white clouds Raphael's, or at least Renaissance art. He wanted it to be dark and cold, the darkness and cold of the valley of the shadow of death. The light was unseemly. His mother had been dead for three weeks, and every day for three weeks he had allowed himself to imagine her letters, letters approving of their lives, approving of him who had caused her pain and madness.

The sixteen-foot steel gate opening into the pasture was painted an industrial red. He pulled the chain off the six-penny nail driven into the gatepost. The chain, touching the gate, sounded like a tuned-down sanctus bell. He went through, fastened the chain again, and walked across the pasture. The roof of the barn shone like polished pewter. From the back the old blue-and-gray tractor resembled a squat, grazing animal with its antlers pointing toward the ground. The tack room, smelling of leather and sweet feed, was separated from the stalls by a wide cement walkway where they washed the horses. He and his son had built this barn. He always felt peaceful here. His mother had not been impressed with his only monument, a still-unfinished barn. He thought of Jozsef Maria dying in an asylum; of Agnes, his beautiful, fearless sister who could fly airplanes and beat him at tennis; and of his mother, who could tell the story of the whole Ring and sing all the individual parts. He thought of the blue airmail letter, the letter of approval he had waited for all his life, that would never come.

The Angel of His Presence

The first time he saw the cobbled courtyard of Hopton Hall's Butler's Quarters in Derbyshire, he imagined hearing the sound of
horseshoes striking the uneven stones, even though the stables were
empty and the carriage house had been converted into an indoor
swimming pool. At home at SolTerra Farms in Alachua, Florida, their
horses walked on a roughened cement walkway between the stalls to
be saddled, backed between the shafts of the two-wheeled sulky,
shoed, washed, and groomed, yet the immanence of the cobbled
courtyard at Hopton Hall seemed to have the power to transform this
unit of Holiday Cottages Group Ltd. into a Masterpiece Theatre pro-
duction of a Jane Austen novel, where the carriages were always immaculate and the drivers always started their beautifully groomed
horses with "Walk on."

Three months ago in May their children had told them about the
plans that had been made for their fiftieth wedding anniversary. The
committee — in addition to their children, it consisted of their closest
English friends living in Sudbury, Derbyshire — had started planning
almost two years ago for the all-important July 8 date. It was in May
that their son John had presented them with first-class plane tickets
and their daughter Sibet, who was compiling a guest list, had shown
them the photo she had selected for the invitation. It was taken in 1950

by a street photographer on Oxford Street who used a London double-decker bus as the background to present Meg striding toward the American Embassy, secure in her dual citizenship, holding tight to her tall, thin, dark, displaced enemy-alien husband. They had been married three months earlier at St. Peter's in Somersal Herbert on the Derbyshire-Staffordshire border. Meg's father had been the vicar of St. Peter's and the rector of All Saints, a much larger church in Sudbury on the Derbyshire side.

"We found this place on the Internet, Daddy. Hopton Hall. It's big enough for all of us, and it's close enough to Sudbury so we wouldn't be taking advantage of our friends by a mass invasion. And it's the ideal place for you. You'll be within walking distance of a church and a pub called The Miners Arms." His son had handed him a faxed sheet.

YOUR LOCATION GUIDE IS AS FOLLOWS

From Ashbourne, take the B5035 and follow the signs for Carsington Water. After the entrance to Carsington reservoir & the Knockerdown pub, take 2nd left to Carsington & Hopton. Into the village and 300 yards past the Miners Arms on the right-hand side is the entrance to Hopton Hall.

"We'll never find it," he had said, remembering being lost while reading a detailed military map of the Donbas on his way to Donetsk with three medium tanks. Donetsk, with a population of almost one million, was a good-sized Soviet town.

Actually it took only three days in Derbyshire for him to feel competent enough to rent a car and drive it on the left-hand side of the road, happily zooming around the narrow, hedge-bordered lanes, shifting down with his left hand as they passed Knockerdown Pub on the way to Ashbourne.

"Could you have imagined fifty years ago driving to an Ashbourne bank in our luxury car to turn a thousand dollars into I don't know how many pounds sterling?" He caught a glimpse of Carsington

Water through the woods on the right. The reservoir glinted in the sun, spotlighting the masts of the tethered sailboats.

"In our *rented* luxury car," Meg said.

"OK. In our *rented* luxury car." As a European Voluntary Worker in 1948, he had earned four pounds a week in a Welsh coal mine, then later three pounds a week in Todmorden, Lancashire, as a four-loom weaver in a cotton mill. He was starving most of the time. At Shenley Mental Hospital in Hartfordshire, where he met Meg, he was paid three pounds a week with room and board. All the unmarried kitchen porters had free rooms above the kitchen and could take baths in the common bathroom. He had hated the place even though he wasn't hungry anymore. Before meeting Meg, he had been invisible in Shenley. Only the chronic patients from behind their chain-link fences and the French nurses walking on the grounds acknowledged his existence, waving and smiling at him. "The first time I saw you was by the huge, oval flower-bed in front of the administration building. You were pushing a bike with a little basket on the handlebars. There were flowers in it."

"I saw you before that when I was on call one Saturday. I had to go to the kitchen for my lunch plate," Meg said. "You were gagging on something."

"It was the smell of the scorched soup on the wall of the boiler. It always made me sick." Balancing on the rim of the boiler with his head inside it and his feet off the floor, he would scrape away the remains of the soup. What kept him going was the knowledge that soon, after the cooks poured hot, soapy water on the tiles, he would be scrubbing the kitchen floor with a long-handled brush, taking his time at the porthole set into the door that led to the medical staff's canteen. He would be watching Meg eating her lunch. Not that he knew her name then, or that she called herself a mongrel for having a South Carolinian mother.

A mud-plastered four-wheel-drive car passed them with a deep roar of its tires.

"I would have made a good bird dog with my sensitive nose," he said, turning on the windscreen washer. "At St. Albans' Gas Works it was my job to shovel sand out of the filter boxes. The gas smell stayed in my nose all the way to Shenley when I walked over to visit you. It was better than being a kitchen porter, though, knowing that when people saw us together they thought I had aspirations above my station."

"I didn't know you walked all that way. I've never known you to walk when you didn't have to. It was eight miles from St. Albans to Shenley."

"Sixteen miles both ways. I didn't have the pennies for the bus fare. If you remember, it was a penny a mile." He turned into the roundabout with no hesitation, like a native.

"No wonder your face was flushed. Sometimes you were shaking like a horse trying to shoo flies away."

"I still had a mild case of malaria. There had been lots of mosquitoes in the swamps around the Donbas before the snow and the thirty below temperatures arrived."

He turned left into a narrow, two-way street where even with cars parked halfway up both sidewalks there was room only for one car to move forward in either direction. "Driving here makes me feel like I'm in a foreign country."

"Thanks to our children we *are* in a foreign country." Meg patted his hand resting on the gearshift lever. "We have so much to be thankful for."

The street widened like a river, flowing around a park, then around a stone church darkened by past emissions from the now-defunct cotton mills with their opaque windows glinting like motionless, blind eyes. The smokeless chimneys were still standing, their red brick shaded by soot transforming these useless symbols of the industrial revolution into something malign, something alien that seemed to be waiting to rule the town again. He remembered as a ten-year-old seeing a slim tower in Budapest and being told that it was Turkish. Without an imam calling the faithful to prayer, the minaret had be-

come a sinister memorial to the hundred and fifty years of Turkish occupation three hundred years ago, with its impalings and beheadings, a
reminder of the Turks' most cruel act: the taking of boys seven and
eight years old, not only robbing them of their families and their religion but also turning them into Janissaries, the most fanatical members of the Ottoman Army. They would be the ones sent back to put
down the periodic insurrections. Stories were still told sixty years ago
about mothers who, recognizing their sons, called the fierce, turbaned,
scimitar-wielding soldiers by their Christian names.

"The parking lot is to the right," Meg said. He couldn't help smiling at the sign that said PAY & DISPLAY, even though Meg would ac-
cuse him of having a dirty American mind. "We'll meet back here at
twelve o'clock," she said.

*   *   *

He watched Meg enter the bakery shop. She was hoping to order sand-
wiches for the small family party they were giving tomorrow at
Hopton Hall's Butler's Quarters. Nothing as simple here as going to a
Publix to order trays of finger food, though he would have gladly
traded their local Publix for a pub. But, as Meg had pointed out, that
was not an option.

The cobblestone street, hemmed in on both sides by shops of all
kinds, rose steeply, the sidewalks opening up like crabs' claws to encir-
cle the Market Place with a war memorial in the middle of it. It was
market day, and there were stalls set up with all sorts of merchandise
heaped on the tables or hung from rafters. On one of the tables he saw
brass harness buckles. Either the price was excessive, or he wasn't able
to adjust yet to the inflation that had occurred during the last ten years.
It was ten years ago that he was measured for his tweed jacket that,
considering the Florida climate, should last his lifetime and beyond as
an inheritance for John-Gray, his eleven-year-old grandson. Meg had
picked out the tweed cloth at Brocklehurst, Town & Country Tradi-

tional Clothing Suppliers. It didn't look like the fabric used in any of the ready-made jackets hanging in the windows of the department stores. She had selected one of the heather blends where blue, rose, and purple in the warp enriched the weave, turning it into a soft, warm gray. It had cost an exorbitant 80 pounds sterling. As a working stiff in Britain from '48 to '50 he had never earned more than 190 pounds a year.

He walked on, noticing the Englishness of the people around him. On the taxi ride from Manchester airport to the train station, the streets had thronged with Pakistanis, Indians, and people from the Caribbean, but here they looked more or less alike — generic English. He would smile at familiar-looking people and receive stony stares in return. Britons were not given to smiling at strangers. In a few more days the ethnicity would dissolve, and he would be able to see them as individual people. It was always the same on each visit, even if this was the only place on earth he was homesick for. While mowing the pastures at SolTerra with his earmuffs on to keep out the noise, he would rehearse in his mind walking this same route in Ashbourne, waving at shopkeepers or sitting with Gareth, the landlord of the Vernon Arms, drinking pints that tasted like proper beer (instead of the ice-cold brew served at home), then looking into the window of the shop that always sold the same statues carved out of coal, unchanged in a world where even the Church's liturgy that people had burned at the stake for had changed not only in its cadences but also in its theology. He wanted to be reassured, even if only by a shop catering to tourists on their way to the Peak District.

And there they were again in the shopwindow: the little locomotives, cars, motorbikes, and miners holding their lamps, all lovingly carved out of deep-black coal, statues that Meg would never allow in their home and his own mother would have dismissed with a wave of her hand. He turned into a newsagent's, not to buy a paper or a magazine from among the multitudes catering to all tastes, but to smell the affable, never-repriseable smell of the place. Just as he always visited the Bass Museum, not really to look at Bass beer's brewing history and to taste their lovely beer (whose bottled image with the red triangle was reproduced by Edouard Manet in his famous *Bar at the Folies-Bergère*), but to visit their nineteen-, twenty-, and even twenty-two-hand shire horses. Walking on Ashbourne's cobblestone sidewalks, he felt an excitement that he was unable to define, that transmitted through the soles of his boots, the identical sensation he had experienced as a boy looking at the copperplate illustrations of his translated Dickens' novels.

He crossed another street, then passed a flower shop that shouldn't have been there, that wasn't there ten years ago, and he realized that Brocklehurst's, the fine clothier that he sought, that he wanted to return to with the fervor of a university alumnus returning for the homecoming game, was nowhere in sight. He was lost again in a strange place. Desperately looking for a familiar sign, anything that would anchor him safely in the present, he leaned against a wall of a building, feeling the rough surface against his back, hoping to slow the onslaught, but nothing could. Feverishly trying to classify the sounds around him, he slipped into a state of hyperalertness; then his autonomic nervous system captured him and took him away to a place he didn't want to go.

*   *   *

The snow was blindingly white, covering the ruins of the small hamlet with only the chimneys visible with their ermine collars. It had been burned down either by the Red Army to deny shelter to the enemy or by the Germans or one of their allies. He himself had never burned down villages or farms, but remembering lectures on denying artillery spotters their perches, he routinely knocked down church steeples with direct cannon fire from his tank. Another lecture from one of his Military Academy classes dealt with the organization of the Army, from the subdivisions into tactical units in the larger corps down to the smallest units still capable of action. Two remaining soldiers of a unit with their weapons intact were counted, on paper at least, as a fighting force, though every commander knew enough to write them off as *enfants perdus*. Three days ago he had become the lone survivor of an explosion that instantly transformed him from a soldier into a toy figurine enclosed in a vast white sphere interspersed with charred ruins and shattered trees, a prisoner in a freezing, immense globe shaken by an impersonal hand that kept the snow swirling so that the tips of his fingers could touch the cold white death all around him. His breath, frozen into narrow icicles, was hanging down from the ski mask that his sister had sent in the summer of '43 for a joke. He was desperately peering at the face of his frozen compass, another humorous gift sent by her to poke fun at his deficient sense of direction. It was a small compass, made for the Boy Scouts to commemorate Lord Baden-Powell's visit in 1933 to the Hungarian Jamboree in Gödölö.

This was the third day since his tank had run over a mine hidden in the snow. They were coming from a depot loaded with legitimate supplies — ammunition, cans of oil and gas, canned food, clothing items — and stolen ones — cases of booze, large boxes of Gillette Blue Blades stolen with an eye to future black-market deals, sheets of sole leather, and a fifty-liter barrel of wine. They stole in good conscience, knowing that the depot would be blown up as soon as the Red Army was fifty kilometers from it, and without fear that the supply personnel would report them. They began to roll at 17:00 hours to rejoin the Second Tank Division. It was already dark. Only an approximate geographical location of the Second Tank Division's whereabouts was given. The division was in what the dispatches called a "fluid situation." He and his crew had been left behind because their tank needed mechanical repairs. They were on their own, slightly drunk, feeling the effects of five days at the depot. Five days without freezing, fear, hunger, without being told to move in a compass direction that any sane person understood would kill them. On arrival at the depot they had been deloused and were allowed to sleep. Slowly he had been rising from the protective depths to a world where he could again remember his mother playing the piano in the music room, a world where Bach and Mozart lived, Saint-Saens, Monteverdi, Vivaldi, Brahms, Albinoni, Palestrina, a world where his mother had the strength to sing the aria *... despairing, I die despairing, and I have never loved life so much, life so much!* from Puccini's opera *Tosca* in his father's hospital room because he had asked for it and for his dress uniform. He wanted to be buried in his uniform and didn't trust his son to place his military medals in the right order without supervision. He was dying from a shrapnel wound at the age of forty-five.

They were rolling in a northwesterly direction with frequent stops because his dysentery had worsened. He had it already at the depot, but trying to cure it with red wine made it worse. There was a full moon by the time they drove cautiously by a small wood. It had stopped snowing. The shadows of the trees on the ground were like black-ink drawings on white paper. They halted for him to clamber down and enter the woods. He had laid down the tommy gun first, then his coat. The cold was numbing, but he had to pull off his gloves because it was difficult to undo the ties on the three sets of long johns he was wearing. He was in agony trying not to soil himself. Afterward he washed with snow, then carefully dried himself. Chafing out here could totally incapacitate a man. He put on his coat, gloves, and was picking up the tommy gun when he heard the tank accelerate and move on. His driver, nicknamed "Taxi" because he had been a taxi driver in Budapest, liked to play games with his lieutenant. Every time he had to get out they would move off, then come back for him, but not before he waved and shouted "Taxi!" The other two were older than he was, married with children, always worrying about their families living on the outskirts of Budapest. They treated him as their mascot, their lucky charm, believing that they were safe with him. Over the last six months they had become his friends, uncles, his family. He had seen photos of their wives, their children, even Peter's vizsla called Ricky. Peter hunted in civilian life. He still did as their loader.

He was walking toward the edge of the woods when he was

knocked down by a wind that made the snow roll over him like an avalanche, burying him before the whoosh of the explosion reached him, then the sound of the ammunition going off in bursts, and he was running toward the flames that were his tank with its cannon and two machine guns. He could smell the cordite and the melting steel of the armor, then the burning flesh, and doubling over was sick into the snow that had become mud. Feeling the heat from the pyre, he stepped back, noticing for the first time the sudden, utter silence. He was deaf. He couldn't hear anything. There was no sound anywhere. He was in a sealed-in globe. The snow began to fall again, covering everything.

*   *   *

He smelled wood smoke but couldn't see where it was coming from. He followed his nose like a bird dog on a scent, moving his soaked legs cautiously: up-over-down, up-over-down, as his father had taught him to do when trying not to spook a covey of quail. Behind him his footsteps curved like the spinal column of a dinosaur in a museum exhibit. He didn't notice when it had stopped snowing. From the air the parallel indentations would be visible a long way off. There would be no sound when a fighter dived on him. Too late he would only see a swooping shadow. Every fifth bullet the plane's machine gun fired was a tracer. He had seen what phosphorous bullets could do to people. The thought of the pain frightened him.

The hut with the smoking chimney wasn't far from where he had stopped. He could visualize the stove and feel the heat that would allow him to stop moving, allow him to lie down and sleep. There could be partisans waiting inside who would turn the hut into his tomb. The Army booklets described what the partisans would do. It was always castration before the killing, but not if he could make his frozen tommy gun work. He should have kept it under his coat. It was still possible to skirt the hut, but where would he go? The little energy he had came from the stolen German Army-issue energy chocolate he had had in his coat pocket. It not only gave him strength to move from the site of the explosion; it also stopped his dysentery.

The door of the hut opened, the warm, steaming air obscuring the gray bundle gesturing toward him to come in. He moved step by slow step, blinking away the falling snow, wondering if he would be entering his own tomb. It had started snowing again. Watching the man's lips move soundlessly, he shook his head to indicate he was deaf and touched his left ear under the fur flap of the winter cap that once belonged to a Red Army officer. The old man, understanding, stretched out his bare hands. He gave the tommy gun to him, remembering his own voice among thirty-two boys in Dr. Mezö's fifth-form Latin class shouting, *Jacta alea est. Jacta alea est.* This was his own crossing of the Rubicon.

"*Come inside, gospodin. I will give you tea.*" The old man spoke slowly so that he could read his lips.

* * *

He woke to the miraculous sounds of snoring and the crackling of wood in the stove. He was lying in a raised alcove that was part of the stove, soaking in the warmth, not remembering how he got up here or who pulled off his boots. His tanker's short leather uniform coat with the sheepskin lining covered his feet. His flannel foot-rags had been washed and were hanging from a string line over the stove. When he first stepped over the threshold and saw a woman standing behind the old man, he wasn't afraid anymore. Her dark-blond hair, not covered with a babushka, was pulled back and tied behind her head. He had looked at her lovely face that wasn't a muzhik's face but the face of the angel that used to hang on the wall beside his bed in the nursery and had felt a rush of unexpected, overwhelming love that nullified the explosion, the smell of burning flesh, and the endlessly white cold that had ruled his world with dizzying hunger. He had wanted to kneel in adoration, but then everything stopped.

He slid down from his warm perch, feeling the cold air on his back. His bare feet touched the reed-covered clay floor. It crackled. The snoring stopped, then started and stopped again. In the silence his footsteps sounded as if somebody was crunching up sheets of paper in angry despair. The door squeaked open. The cold snow was a shock to his feet. He urinated just a few steps to the side of the door, then came back in. The old man, standing beside the stove with his hands stretched over it, was waiting for him.

"*Bread and tea for you.*" He spoke slowly, looking up into his face.

"*I can hear,*" and touching his ears, he shouted again. "*I can hear.*"

"*You speak Russian!*"

"*A little.*"

"*Elosia,*" the old man shouted. "*He speaks Russian.*"

The woman emerged from behind a gray blanket stretched across the back of the hut. She had braided her hair and coiled it around her head. It looked like the crowns of the saints on the icons. He felt like a penitent in her presence.

"*Elosia, bring the bread,*" the old man said. "*You sit down.*"

He sat down on one of the crudely made chairs next to the table. Elosia came with the bread and a pottery dish filled with salt and placed them on the table, then went to the samovar. She filled three thick glasses with tea, put them on the table, and sat down.

"*Are you German?*" the old man asked.

"*No. Hungarian. Ungaro.*"

"*Ungaro.*" The old man lifted a loaf of flat, round bread and wedged it against his chest. Then, taking a long-bladed knife from the table, he made the sign of the cross on it and cut a slice for each of them.

"*Eat, Ungaro.*" The old man sprinkled salt on his slice of bread. "*This is our last loaf. Andrei Konstantinovich should have come a week ago.*"

"*You give last bread to enemy?*" He pointed to his own chest. "*Enemy. Ungaro.*"

"*Ungaro,*" the old man said, "*how can we receive the Heavenly Bread if we don't give you earthly bread? Eh?*"

"*Heavenly Bread*," Elosia said, crossing herself. "*Vi paneemayetye?*" She had a sweet voice that contrasted with the old man's growly speech.

"*Come, Ungaro,*" the old man said. "*I'll show you.*"

Elosia pulled back the blanket-curtain. Against the side wall on the top of a small altar covered with a white sheet stood a triptych. The old man and Elosia stepped toward it. She reached back for his hand. The brief contact felt as if he had been embraced. They knelt and crossed themselves. He did the same.

"*For the peace of God and the salvation of our souls,*" the old man prayed. "*Thou who reconciled earth to heaven through Thine only-begotten Son, grant that we, who by the darkness of our sins turned aside from brotherly love, may by Thy light shed forth in our souls, embrace our enemies, this Ungaro,*" he pointed behind him with his thumb, "*and that he embrace us in mutual affection through Jesus Christu, thy Son, our Lord and our most holy, pure, blessed, and glorious Lady, the Theotokos and ever-virgin Mary with all the saints, let us commit ourselves and one another and our whole life to Christ our God.*"

They stayed on their knees awhile, then stood up. Elosia pulled across the blanket-curtain and genuflected.

"*Vi paneemayetye, Ungaro?*" the old man said.

"*Paneemayetye.*" He didn't know all the words, but he did understand. The old man stepped closer and embraced him.

"*You are a good man, Ungaro,*" the old man said and, reaching up, made the sign of the cross on his forehead. He was patting the old man's back, crying. Today was his twenty-first birthday. He had been given his life as a present.

Two days later in the afternoon there was a knock on the door of the hut and a man entered. He had a scar that cut his left ear in half and pulled up the corner of his lip into a sneer. He had a sack on his shoulder. Seeing a stranger, the man reached into the sack.

"No," the old man shouted. "*No, Andrei Konstantinovich. You, Ungaro, go and pray.*" He pantomimed prayer with his hands.

From behind the curtain he listened to their voices. They were growling, barking at each other in short sentences. Andrei Konstantinovich, dressed partly in uniform items that must have been taken from dead soldiers, looked like a partisan. He heard Elosia's voice and the laughter that followed it. Her sweet voice filled him with longing. He wanted to belong in their community. He wanted to stay here, away from the war. There was more talk; then the old man called.

"*Come here, Ungaro.*"

He stepped out from behind the curtain. Elosia was putting away the contents of the sack.

"*This is our Ungaro, Andrei Konstantinovich. A good man. When it gets dark you will take him to where the other Ungaros are so he can go home.*"

They ate bread and cured bacon and drank small glasses of vodka. When it got dark, Elosia took the white sheet off the altar and covered him with it. Andrei Konstantinovich had refused to walk with a "crow" who could be seen from a hundred versts. The old man blessed him and gave him back his tommy gun.

It was very cold outside. After a few steps he turned back to look at Elosia and the old man for the last time. When he turned back the second time, the hut was invisible. He was thinking that he was Lazarus still covered in his shroud, going out into the world.

*   *   *

He was standing at a street corner beside a traffic light, looking across the street at the shiny brass plaque of the Ashbourne Westminster Bank Ltd. It was the same type of plaque used on the interior walls of churches to memorialize people and events. He remembered some wit telling him that the brass plaques had turned Westminster Abbey into a better-class pawnshop. A large lorry was hurtling down the street to beat the traffic light. A woman who must have been standing just behind him was stepping into its path. He reached out and pulled her back. "Seeing you flattened by that lorry, madam, would have ruined my fiftieth wedding anniversary celebration," he said by way of an explanation.

"Sorry." She smiled. "I was in too much of a hurry." She was a tall blond woman dressed in trousers and tunic that vaguely resembled a uniform. They crossed the street together.

"May I ask your assistance?" He wanted to sound like a properly polite native.

"Certainly. One good deed deserves another."

"I am lost."

"I know."

"Could you direct me toward the Market Place, please."

"Of course."

She led him through small alleyways he had never seen before; then they came to a larger street that swelled into a circle fronted with shops. A street musician, a violinist, was playing a Chopin waltz in front of a shopwindow filled with stuffed animals. When they were little, his grandchildren had treasured their stuffed "aminals." They still did, even though in two years, Kate, who was fourteen, would be old enough to drive, and John-Gray, at eleven, was already driving a riding mower with a trailer to take salt blocks to the horses. Just before leaving for England, Sarah, who would soon be seven, had insisted that she no longer needed training wheels on her bike.

"Am I walking too fast for you?"

"Oh, no. I am sorry to have taken you out of your way."

"You didn't," she said, pointing. Across the street was the bakery shop.

"Thank you. You can't imagine how much you helped me," he said, but the woman had disappeared. Meg was coming down the bakery steps holding on to the railing.

"Meg!" He embraced her. "I'm so glad I found you again. I got lost."

"Did you find Brocklehurst's?"

"No. I think they moved."

"It took longer at the bakery than I anticipated," Meg said. "You look tired. Let's have a cup of tea and a bite to eat. The bakery is also a café." She started back up the bakery steps.

"I wonder if angels are always blond?" he said.

*   *   *

He came off an A road with the help of two roundabouts and crossed a narrow bridge that led into a lane that barely accommodated the width of the car yet had the power to transport him back fifty years. He was walking here in the moonlight on July 7, 1950, toward Somersal Hall, a glorious Elizabethan house built in 1502 that had been his official address for the reading of the banns. He was to spend his final bachelor night in Somersal Hall as the guest of the FitzHerberts, a brother and sister, both unmarried, the last of their line. St. Peter's, the church he was to be married in, was right next to Somersal Hall.

He let down the windows to hear better. A head-on collision was an ever-present danger here. Only the arbitrarily placed lay-bys allowed the locals and the occasional brave outsider to pass in one or the other direction.

"I don't know how the buses manage on these roads."

"That reminds me," Meg said. "While I was in the post office in Sudbury, I heard that the bus service from Somersal Herbert had been discontinued. I wonder how they'll do their shopping."

"I can't remember this left bend." He shifted down into third.

"I can. I used to drive here with Father several days a week when he took the services at St. Peter's. In a minute we'll pass Somersal Hall. Gladys and her husband live in one of the church cottages. They'll give us the church key. You can pull in here."

He remembered the tall, elaborately roofed churchyard gate towered over by a huge beech tree. A slight wind made the pale green leaves sigh, the sigh accompanied by the discrete castanets of some dead branches. He was suddenly aware of the presence of people long gone.

"Meg," he said.

"I know." She came close to him. "I know."

He was conscious of a history that had begun with the two of them in a world that had not existed before their meeting, a world that would cease to exist after they departed, a world filled with pain, crying, sorrow, fear — and love, a poor but glorious imitation of the redeeming Love that had made possible, in spite of everything, the overwhelming joy of the earth.

"I'd better go and get the key from Gladys," Meg said.

Gladys was an old woman with gray-blond hair pulled back and fastened on the top of her head. Her sweet face had retained its youthful beauty, softened only by an inner light that made him want to embrace her before thinking the better of it. At the time of their wedding this nice old Derbyshire country woman had been an unmarried girl of seventeen, ten years younger than himself. And though every morning when he looked in the bathroom mirror he knew definitely that not only could he not hop onto a running horse but that he would need a derrick even to mount one, he never felt old.

"Come in, then," Gladys said, opening the church door. She bent her head slightly to one side like an artist who, after removing the shroud from her art, watched for reactions.

"I almost forgot how lovely it was," Meg said.

"I still remember Mr. Jeffery's prizewinning delphiniums in the windows. Before your wedding he would cut them only for flower shows."

"I still feel bad about it," Meg said. "I went to ask Mr. Jeffery for delphiniums, and when he said it was all right I cut several basketsful. I didn't know that they were his famous prizewinners."

Standing at the back of the church by the many-colored bellpull and the pine table where he had signed their marriage certificate, he looked toward the altar. The nave was lit by the sun coming through the plain, leaded glass windows, making the tops of the pews look like so many horizontal banisters polished by the continuous touch of hands. The gray stone floor showed a shallow indentation, as if a living stream of water flowed between the altar and the people.

At their last visit ten years ago, Mr. Nash, the senior warden, had complained about having to move the altar.

"The Rector showed me the letter from the Bishop of Derby himself," Mr. Nash had said. "After five centuries they tell us to move the altar forward to make room for the priest behind it! You need a shoehorn to get him in there. If we'd moved the altar one more inch, it would have tumbled down on the steps. And then they started mucking about with the liturgy."

Mr. Nash was five or six years older than he was. Through the years they saw each other only when he and Meg came to visit, but in spite of that he loved the smallish man with the weather-beaten face of a yeoman farmer. The cowlick in his still-brown hair belonged on the head of a schoolboy. His calloused, oversized hands were like tools that he used gently, hesitatingly when shaking hands. There was a straightforward openness in him, decency that radiated like a beacon and made everybody trust him. In the Nashes' rather untidy kitchen was a photograph of a smiling HRH Prince Charles standing next to Mr. Nash in that same untidy kitchen. Most of the villagers, seeing the photograph, were embarrassed. They thought that Mrs. Nash should have tidied up, but Mrs. Nash didn't know that Prince Charles was coming to change his britches in her kitchen and put on his riding togs. It was all for the prince's safety that he would leave his residence in street clothes, then get into the helicopter that would take him to Derbyshire to ride one of the string of hunters that he kept at an undisclosed location. Prince Charles and his detectives trusted Mr. Nash never to reveal the time or the date of the visit. Mr. Nash never did, even to his wife.

"How is Mr. Nash keeping these days, Gladys?"

"Didn't Audrey or one of the girls write you? . . . Mr. Nash died in March," Gladys said. "Come on. I'll show you."

The day had not changed. It was just as lovely outside as when he had entered St. Peter's. The July grass still reminded him of Watteau's landscapes with their orderly, mowed lawns. Gladys's husband Oliver tended the churchyard with its trees, bushes, flowers, and gravestones, as his father had done before him.

"They are all here," Gladys said.

They were all there. Mr. Nash's father and grandfather with their wives. Babes and young children dying from illnesses that were cured now with ease, young women dying in childbirth, and always the young men, the lads, dying in wars, battles, skirmishes in faraway places, their bodies no longer trapped in sunken ships or foreign soils. Here in St. Peter's churchyard death had lost its terror, its impersonal awfulness. The people either praised God inside the church or rested outside, awaiting the sound of the trumpet blast in blessed certainty. For a farmer like Mr. Nash, the soil of Somersal Herbert was as familiar as his own body. The last conversation he had with Mr. Nash was about planting his crops.

"I was instructed by the EU," Mr. Nash had said, "and that's Brussels, mind you, not to plant closer than six feet from my hedges."

"How would they know?" He was sitting on the same lumpy leather couch Prince Charles must have sat on.

"They have satellites to spy on us."

"You must be joking! This is England."

"We stopped Adolph, but what do you do when your own government fancy the notion? They want to turn us into a bloody global village! There won't be such a thing as England. My dad wanted to take a strap to me just for reading *Brave New World*. What would he think now?"

Mr. Nash was safe, secure in his Englishness, resting here among his family, friends, and neighbors. Beyond the churchyard, across a sunken road, two hedges came together in an L joined by an iron cattle gate where a young Angus bull stood, looking at him.

"And what do you think about the world, young bull?" he said. The bull shook his head, then with a snort turned his back on him.

Every action, every idea brings with it unforeseen consequences, he thought, like the waves caused by a rock hurled into a pond. In the

eighteenth century Rousseau had hurled his rock. The immediate consequence of that was the French Revolution, where the idea of liberty
and equality gave rise to people-butchers who wanted to burn down li-
braries because they believed that all requisite knowledge was already
deposited in the Revolution. In the end, what the guillotine achieved
was a new emperor. Now again the same waves caused by that same
rock were lapping on the shores of the land of the Magna Carta.

In school he had to memorize Rousseau's definition of dependency. *Liberty, because every particular dependency is that much power taken by
force from the body of the State, and equality, because liberty cannot exist without
it.* Rousseau advocated breaking the "particular" dependency that re-
sides in the family and substituting a faceless international community, *la volonte generale,* that in its promise of unity would replace the
family with what Hannah Arendt described as an "atomistic mass."
The Piarist fathers never forgot to mention that Rousseau had turned
over his own children to public welfare.

Inside the church Gladys and Meg were still talking. He went to
the back, to the pine table where he had signed the marriage certificate.
He wanted to reach for the bellpull to announce to the world that he
was here in consequence of seeing a girl more than fifty years ago by
an oval flower-bed pushing a bike that had a basket of wildflowers on
the handlebars. But he didn't ring the bell. It would only bring Oliver
over here to find out what all the commotion was about.

*   *   *

The flowers against the background of St. Peter's leaded, diamond-
patterned clear-glass windows stood out like so many still lives created
with thick oil-paint, where each solid color blended simply because of
its position in the arrangement. The deep-blue delphiniums dominating the pale-yellow lupines and the white Queen Anne's lace focused
the eye for a moment before the lavender Canterbury bells, purple
buddleia, and foxgloves came into sight among the white syringa and

the white and blue scabious. There were also flowers in the font and in the cast-iron vases attached to the walls. Here the same flowers differently arranged made him think of coats of arms with their crest, mantling, and quartered escutcheon. These too were the same flowers that Meg had arranged fifty years ago with her mother and her sister Mary. Mary was here again. She had come from Virginia with her husband, children, and a first grandchild. His own beloved Mamsie, his mother-in-law, without a doubt was looking down anxiously (as anxious as it was possible for a soul to be) to make certain everything was right, beautiful, and above all proper. (It was she who had taught him that in England one never ever butters toast on the palm of one's hand and that one measures rum into a teaspoon before adding it to one's tea.)

Gwyneth, the youngest of Meg's sisters, was seven years old when they got married in 1950. Yesterday Gwyneth was the main flower arranger with Meg. She was now draping their father's clerical cape on the end of the pew. The family was always great for symbolism.

"I shouldn't be sitting next to you," Kate said.

"Why not? You are my oldest grandchild."

"This is your fiftieth anniversary. Grandmamma should be sitting next to you."

"Where is she?" Then he saw her pushing Gwyneth's old nanny in a wheelchair toward the front pew. Kate moved over to make room for her grandmother.

"I thought we had lost you," he said.

"I helped with Elaine's wheelchair."

Sarah, who sat the furthest from them, leaned forward and wiggled her fingers at her grandmother.

"I see you," Meg said. "Do you like the flower arrangements?"

"They are beautiful, Grandmamma."

"I like the deep blues next to the pale-yellow ones," John-Gray said.

There was a note from the organ. The congregation rose with the sound of a great collective sigh and began to sing.

Praise, my soul, the King of Heaven, to his feet thy tribute bring; Ransom'd, heal'd, restored, forgiven, evermore His praises sing: Alleluia! Alleluia! Praise the everlasting King.

They had come to celebrate this marriage that by God's grace had lasted fifty years. They were Anglicans for the most part, church people who knew the hymnal and liked to sing, experiencing the joy of the psalmist: *"Blessed is the people who know the joyful sound: they shall walk, O Lord, in the light of thy countenance."* He looked at Meg's face, slightly tilted toward the heavens as she sang.

Father-like, He tends and spares us; well our feeble frame He knows; In His hand He gently bears us, rescues us from all our foes: Alleluia! Alleluia! Widely yet His mercy flows.

Hearing a sweet soprano voice coming from one of the pews behind him, he realized that a door in heaven was opened a crack for him to behold that which was to come: a place for them to gather where love, forgiveness, and peace sang, where hurt, pain, anger, and bad dreams were no more.

Angels in the height, adore Him; ye behold Him face to face; Saints triumphant, bow before Him, gather'd in from every race: Alleluia! Alleluia! Praise with us the God of grace.

The priest, a slight man in a white cassock standing in front of the altar, raised his arms.

"Let us pray," he said.

*　　　*　　　*

After the reading of the Collect for the third Sunday after Trinity, his son John, who sat with his wife in the pew behind them, stood up. He felt the touch of John's hand on his shoulder, then watched him, a tall, curly headed man, walk up the aisle to stand behind the lectern on the Epistle side of the altar, remembering the curly headed boy (still blond, before his hair had turned dark at the age of eleven) standing at the Epistle side of their homemade altar, reading the appropriate lesson for the day appointed in the lectionary for Evensong. He loved his son's voice. It made it possible for him to accept the fact that for the rest of his life he would speak with an accent no matter which language he spoke. The altar had been built out of three old steamer trunks stacked on each other and covered with an old carpet and the fair linen his own mother had sent from Hungary. Meg had created a pottery censer that hung from the ceiling by Sibet's braided cord. He had made the oak altar-cross from a broken picture frame. The altar was in perfect scale for the dimensions of the storage room at one end of the back porch that their children had turned into St. Francis's chapel, named after Edward Francis, their English grandfather. There was not much room in the chapel because of the dogs. The children's argument for the presence of the dogs was the example of Exeter Cathedral, where a sign outside the doors simply stated, "Put on leash, please."

There was one Evensong he would always remember. John had read from the third chapter of the book of Habakkuk. He himself had been standing at the Gospel side of the altar. *Lord, I have heard of your fame,* John had read, *I stand in awe of your deeds, O Lord. Renew them in our day, in our time make them known.*

Looking at his son, hearing him read this passage, he had been jolted as if by lightning so that he had to reach out to hold onto the altar for support to endure the intense silver light that had banished all the shadows, showing the shabbiness of the storage room. He had felt naked, insignificant, dependent like a little child, and like a child he did not question the light, accepting it as if he had always known that signs were posted for the benefit of the weak and shortsighted who were trying to find their way through the jumble of life.

"Here beginneth the first reading from the First Epistle of the Apostle Peter, chapter five, verses six to eleven."

John had a pleasing baritone voice now, but the boy he remembered was still there when he smiled or when he was moved close to tears.

"Humble yourselves therefore under the mighty hand of God, that he may

exalt you in due time: Casting all your care upon him; for he careth for you. Be so-
ber, be vigilant; because your adversary the devil, as a roaring lion, walketh about,
seeking whom he may devour: Whom resist steadfast in the faith, knowing that
the same afflictions are accomplished in your brethren that are in the world. But
the God of all grace, who hath called us unto his eternal glory by Christ Jesus, af-
ter that ye have suffered a while, make you perfect, stablish, strengthen, settle you.
To him be glory and dominion for ever and ever. Amen. Here endeth the first
reading."

*   *   *

Kneeling on the altar steps with his family to receive the Eucharist that
united them with all their flesh and blood, the quick and the dead, men
and women, some of whom fell asleep in ripe old age in their own beds,
children who died under bombed-out houses, young men who died on
battlefields or were lost forever in prisoner-of-war camps, and some
who were squashed like roaches against walls by khaki-colored military
trucks for their transgressions, to have their blood staining the walls su-
persede their lives for weeks, months, and sometimes even for years.
Reaching for the cup, he felt his tears and closed his eyes. His right hand
touched the bottom of the chalice, then he tasted the wine and beheld
Him once more, beheld His Glory that enveloped his own insignificant,
vulnerable self with love that made him realize that God, the Lord of the
Universe, was striving to get through to his finite consciousness so that
he would know that ultimately nothing else mattered.

Back in the pew he prayed wordlessly, for his gratitude went beyond words. There was a time when he had repeated, mantra-like, *Why
me, Lord, why me, Lord, why am I alive?* since his own life seemed too small
a weight on the scales to balance the dead weight of people he had
known for years, months, or sometimes only hours, whose faces and
names he could barely recall, who had become shadows he wanted
desperately to hold on to, as if that could give them continuity to parallel his own ongoing life. Then forty-eight years ago a nurse had placed

his newborn baby girl in his arms, and instinctively he had lifted her up and offered her the safety and love of God. At that moment he had realized that it wasn't his duty to hold on to the dead.

Sitting back on the pew, he watched people move forward. Some of them stopped for a moment to touch his hand or shoulder, then moved on with the stream flowing toward the altar. There was another altar he would always remember. That altar had been hidden behind a curtain made of blankets. It had a triptych on the white sheet that covered it, and there was Elosia, with the face of the angel that used to hang on the wall beside his bed in the nursery, and the old man, whose name he never knew. A little tatterdemalion of a man who had given him life as a present for his twenty-first birthday, and who in the midst of all that hate and killing prayed for the peace of God and for brotherly love. He finally understood why the partisan with the horrible, scarred face had guided him toward his own division instead of killing him. The man's hate for him was as visible as the trees with their naked branches lifted in mute lamentation toward the white sky that he could almost touch, yet Andrei Konstantinovich had risked his own life to deliver him because the old man told him to do so. The old man was a *yourodivyje*.

"*Yourodivyje*," Andrei Konstantinovich had said. "*Vi paneemayetye yourodivyje?*" but he didn't understand, didn't know the meaning of the word till this morning while he was waiting for Meg to finish dressing. He had picked up a travel magazine left open on the windowsill of their room in Hopton Hall's Butler's Quarters. The article highlighted Nizhni Novgorod among other historical points of interest. It had first been destroyed by Ivan the Terrible in the sixteenth century because he had believed on no real evidence that the city pledged cooperation with the Poles to overthrow him. On his orders thousands were massacred, homes and farms were destroyed, and monasteries were sacked. Nobody dared to stand against him other than Nicholas of Pskov, who upbraided the Czar, then slapped a piece of bloody meat into his hand. And the Czar of all the Russians had halted his rampage. Nicholas of Pskov was a *yourodivyje*, a fool in Christ, a man living in total abnegation of the self. His own *yourodivyje* lived in the twentieth century amidst the running tide of killings and hate, praying for the peace of God for all.

The congregation was praying, their voices blending into a single note full of gladness and love for the Word made flesh that dwelt among them. He looked at Meg's sweet profile, the angel whose presence announced His Presence in his own life and who made it possible for him to trust again and to love without counting costs.

They stood up to sing the closing hymn.

He who would valiant be 'gainst all disaster, let him in constancy follow the Master. There's no discouragement shall make him once relent his first avowed intent to be a pilgrim.

Since, Lord, Thou dost defend us with Thy Spirit, we know we at the end shall life inherit. Then fancies fly away! I'll fear not what men say, I'll labor night and day to be a pilgrim.

Acknowledgments

The works in this volume appeared previously in the following publications:

"The Acceptable Time": *Reformed Journal*, vol. 36, no. 3, March 1986

"The Barbershop on Kärtner Strasse": *Tampa Tribune-Times*, 2 July 1995

"A Bearer of Divine Revelation": *Perspectives*, vol. 9, no. 5, May 1994

"Pictures in a Cigar Box": *Image: A Journal of the Arts & Religion*, no. 12, Winter 1995-96

"Waxworks": *Reformed Journal*, vol. 39, no. 4, April 1989

"An Act of Admiration," "The Binge," "Brandenburg Concerto," and "A Slow, Soft River" were published in *A Slow, Soft River* (Eerdmans, 1973).

"At a Certain Angle," "A D-minor Fugue," "Lazarus," "The Noise Was Heard Afar Off," and "Vladimir's Kitchen" were published in *A Slight Momentary Affliction.* Copyright © 1987 by Lawrence Dorr. Reprinted by permission of Louisiana State University Press.